T0198724

ELEVEN YEARS LATER

THE WAY IT IS

JOAN DAVIS

authorHOUSE®

AuthorHouse™
1663 Liberty Drive
Bloomington, IN 47403
www.authorhouse.com
Phone: 1 (800) 839-8640

Published by AuthorHouse 08/09/2018

ISBN: 978-1-5462-3376-3 (sc)
ISBN: 978-1-5462-3375-6 (e)

Library of Congress Control Number: 2018903457

Print information available on the last page.

Contents

CHAPTER 1

(Short Stories)

We often say "if I had it to do all over again, I would do things differently." These are some of the thoughts that has gone through Jeneen's head in the last eleven years. She thought of how much further she could have been in her life, if she had not fallen prey to worldly things. Drugs, alcohol, and money, just to name a few, and it caused her misery over eleven years ago. Well, the past is the past, and she has not dwelled on it, "no condemnation."

However; since then, Jeneen has made a full recovery from her past, and is living a very good life with Mitch, her finance, and they've made plans to get married in 2009. In the past eleven years, Jeneen has thought often about how she became entangled in the web that took so many years of her life. It's not that she living in the past, but it is not easy to let the past rest when it's showing up everyday, in the newspapers, on television, and everyday in her neighborhood. It is a constant reminder of the fact that, even though she has changed, there is still a lot of the world out there that have not. Drugs are still as bad as ever everywhere.

When we make mistakes in our lives, we make statements, such as, "if I knew then, what I know now," or "if I knew that would have happened I would not have gone there." It is not intended for us to see into the future, or predict a certain incident just before in happens. Our minds are not built for that kind of thinking. However; God intends for us to use the common sense that he has given to us to make sound, rational decisions.

Lately it seems there is a lot of action first, and thinking about it later, which is always too late.

It's as though children around the world has not been thinking at all. They have been acting on instinct, and it has caused the gang activity to increase 6.7 per cent in the last eleven years. The crimes that has been committed over the last few years is in some way related to drugs. If not drugs, then by a jealous boy friend, or a retaliating father, husband, or someone that wants to punish that wife or mother, by killing the kids, or raping their own daughters, or sons, and that makes young people turn on their parents.

Do one child shoot another child because of what happens in the home? Have we as parents missed the mark by such a wide margin when it came to our children? Some how, along the way, we didn't dot an "I", or crossed a "T". How could we have missed such a drastic change in our children? The way they dress, the way they talk, the friends they hang out with, and the places they go, are all factors in non communication with our kids.

Jeneen thought back to when she was raising her own children, she remembered asking her children for the telephone numbers of all the children they hung out with, just as a precaution. It is obviously not a major deal for many parents today. Maybe it's too much trouble. Maybe they don't want their child to think that they're prying, or that it would embarrass him, or her too much to ask such private questions. Well picture this if you would mom, or dad; what if your child goes out with a group of boys, and not tell you where they're going, and something happens to your child? It is often too late for the hind sight too set in. "If I only questioned him a little more? Or, you began to wonder if there was a sign you should have noticed. There are signals that children send everyday, it's just that we're so busy with our own lives, that we don't take the time to notice. We have to start noticing the clothing they wearing to school, and what's in their pack sack. Some how these children are smuggling weapons to school, weather in their pack sacks, or in their clothing. With the over sized pants, and shirts, it is almost impossible to see the imprint of their bodies, and even more impossible to spot a weapon of any kind. Aside from all the metal detectors that has been installed in schools around the world, we as parents have to do our part and become detectives to our children before they even leave home, just so they'll know that we're aware of what's happening.

Eleven years ago when Jeneen started her life over, she didn't know what to expect, as far as "how society would treat her," especially those folks that knew her when she was out there on drugs. She knew that most people could be cruel when it came to starting a new life in the same town, but Jeneen had God, will power, and determination. She knew that world improvement could begin with her. She started with her know- ledge of how to deal with the youth, and how to make their lives a little less stressful, and a little less complicated. We have to try and improve the world around them, teach them to love themselves, and eventually they will learn to love others. It is not what you say to young people, but how you say it that will get their attention, and earn their respect. Children are not machines that you create and toss to the side. They need love, attention, and nurturing. You cannot let them raise themselves, doing whatever they want to do, and when they become teenagers you begin trying to direct them by telling them what you think they should do. Well; by then its too late, they've already become a catastrophe, an utter failure, and there's no easy fix for the situation. Their mind is already focused on the ways of the world. However; a child's life is too valuable to let go to waste, that's when you give it one last jolt with a serious shot of tough love. You can give love when there is nothing else left to give, no more money, no more advice, or anything else that you've tried in the pass that has not worked.

The task that's put before us today is to instill in our children's minds that every age is too important to waste, and that God has a plan for their lives. It's childhood, youth, middle age, and then old age, in that order. But, today our children are going from childhood, to middle age, and not living long enough to see old age. Their youth is replaced with drugs, jail, or death. Every one makes mistakes, but the smart young man would not make the same mistake twice. For some reason that does not hold true for these young men today. Maybe it's something about being in jail that pumps them up, because, they constantly make the same mistakes over, and over again just to go back to jail. In spite of all of man's mistakes; the one thing in man's favor is the ability to learn from them. However; learning seems to be an impossible task for children today. They're either kicked out of school for being disobedient, dropping out of school, or having to deal with teachers that solicits young children, and with the teacher's track record, it's a wonder children are still interested in getting an education. However; there are still some teachers that are trying very hard to gain the trust and respect of their students in order to give them a good education.

Jeneen was having her car serviced one day, and just happened to notice a young boy sitting on a trailer at the garage. She looked over at him and asked him his name, as it turned out, he was the son of the mechanic working on her car. She asked him why was he not in school, at 10:00 am in the morning? His answer was "I was kicked out of school." She asked him what reason was he kicked out. He said "I did not like the way the teacher talked to me, so I talked nasty right back to her," and now he is home bound for the rest of the school year. He is only in the sixth grade.

Jeneen could not believe what she heard, and proceeded to give the young boy some advice on the importance of school, and listening to his teacher. She told him that "school is not for the teacher, it is however; for him, and if he was doing what he should have been doing, the teacher would not have scold him without cause". She also explained that "without an education it would be almost impossible for him to get a decent job anywhere, or he could end up in jail, or dead". That was just one of many children that has been kicked out of school, and Jeneen was glad she got the opportunity to tell that child where he would eventuality end up if he don't get his act together, and stay in school. Our young people has to know that they are our future, that they are the head, and not the tail. They are the beginning and not the end. We need to let them know that years could pass and leave them behind.

Eleven years ago, Jeneen was on the inside looking out. From that point of view, she had thoughts of never seeing the world on the other side again. She was in the mist of all the evil, the steeling, the manipulating, the murders, and the drug dealings. Her world was merely black and white, and her reach was no farther than the tip of her fingers. Jeneen never thought that she would survive that ordeal and live to write about it. However; she survived that world, but the world she's now in for eleven years is no better, matter of fact it has gotten worse. The young men are more corrupt than ever, and they still have no problem killing another person to get their fifteen minutes of fame as their pictures are posted everywhere as the city's most wanted. There is not a day that goes by that the head lines does not read "murder by a black young man". Jeneen did not read this one day, but everyday it was something about our young black men committing some offensive act.

It's as if they're possessed by a death demon, and they're destine to die at a very early age. We all know that death is not a distant anxiety that will not sit around and wait for old age. It is a constant thought that haunts us all. We are especially fearful for our children when death is happening so early. Shooting someone at the blink of an eye, is as easy as changing their cloths, and they have no remorse when they do it.

The hope that parents have for their children in today's world seem to be false hope. It's as if parents have actually given up on raising their children. They some how feel defeated. Some are wondering how can we compete with all the laws that has been put in place to protect our children? even from us, their parents. Mothers cannot be the kind of mother that their mothers were. Children don't want to listen, take advice, or to be told what to do, and because of that they're falling by the way side everyday at a younger age.

They tend to make decisions based on peer pressure, circumstances, likes and dislikes, and what mood they are in at the moment. All of it cause fatigue, and stress, which leads to fights, and fights leads to murder, and when murder happens, not only is one life wasted, but there are two or more lives that hangs in the balance. Some how our children has lost their purpose, and direction for their lives.

We can help our children by putting their values above our own. Instead of letting them choose the outfit that you're paying for (which cost way too much), help them to choose something that is just as appealing, but cost a lot less. Do it in a way to where they feel that they've actually made the choice. It is called reverse psychology. I'm sure you all used reversed psychology in some form of your life. It's not hard to do.

Some children find the bigger values in things such as cars, jewelry, drugs, even in their friends, and some of them are willing to die rather than change their ideas. We must help our children change their priorities. We need to teach them to plan for a purpose, and put purpose into their planning.

CHAPTER 2

Making an effort

Have you ever stop to think what it is that make these young folks tick? What cause them to commit the hennas acts that they do? We know it's the work of the devil, and his job is to seek and destroy, and he is killing off our young people in bulks. What we have to do is make more of an effort to communicate with young folks. Let's try talking to them, and not at them. We should try reaching out, asking them what's on their minds, and not tell them what they should think about. We should offer them advice, and not force it upon them (*rather they like it or not*). When an idea is forced upon a child, it's cause for retaliation, or resentment on the child's part.

The time has come for us to change our way of dealing with our children today. We may even have to start thinking the way they think, or put ourselves on their level. God has instilled enough wisdom, and knowledge into our heads as parents so that we can deal with our children on all levels. However; what we cannot handle, we can take it to God, and he will work it out for us.

God knows, in some cases, it will take a strong minded person with a strong will to get through to these children today. A person must also be equipped with Job's patience, the strength of Goliath, and the love of Jesus in your heart, to even start a conversation with any child today.

One day Jeneen decided to drive around town, just to see how the children was spending their summer afternoons while school was out. She even drove to her old neighborhood, which has been turned into an apartment complex. But there are still children living in the area. Her mind went back to the fun times they use to have when school was out. They use to play games such as red light, hopscotch, Simon says, jumping rope, etc. Those were true childhood games that can never be replaced in your mind if you grew up in that era.

As she continued to drive, she saw two, or three young girls, no more than fourteen, or fifteen years of age, pushing baby strollers, pulling a baby by the hand, or pregnant, and fighting with the "baby's daddy" about another girl, who may also be pregnant from the same boy. Although Janeen did not exactly know what the fight was about, but judging from what she overheard, it sound a lot like "I know you are not her baby's daddy too?"

Jeneen drove on a little further thinking "when I was fourteen, I was still playing with baby dolls, serving tea out of plastic tea cups & saucers, with plastic tea pots, dressing paper dolls, and making mud pies." She did not see one child jumping rope, or playing any child hood games. It's as if children has been completely stripped of their youth. There are still some children riding bikes, but for the most part, some ride bikes because is helps them to distribute their drugs faster, being they're too young to drive, that is their only form of transportation. Janeen remembered that from her days in the drug world.

When we think back in time, and remember the way things use to be. It seems the world has completely changed. It's like every thing is working backwards, going in the opposite direction. For example children are not trying to stay in school, they are putting more effort in dropping out of school. Parents aren't running their homes anymore, children are, for the most part. People are not trying to live anymore they are trying desperately to end their lives, and take other people with them. As it is said in Ephesians 5:14 "Awake them that sleeps, arise from the dead for it is time to live again in Jesus." God is not sleeping he is awake and waiting for us to come to him asking blessing for our young people.

CHAPTER 3

Understanding our Youth

Understanding our young people, is not as hard as it is to get them to understand what it is we're trying to teach them. Understanding starts with listening, thinking, and comprehending what you hear. We as a person, or as a parent are a weak personal. We cannot handle rejection very well. No! is not a word we want in our vocabulary, because it is an ego crusher. There is an old saying that "time changes all things, and that we must change with the time," and that is true, because we now have a black president of the United States, and his campaign slogan was, "It is time for a change."

I'm sure Dr. Martin Luther King Jr. is looking down from heaven with a big smile on his face because of what we as black people have accomplished. That's right we have over come, and we still have a long way to go yet, in regards to the way some folks still feel about black folks. They still feel that "this is a white mans world and a white president should run the country". It does not matter how many interracial couples appear in society today, it will not change the way a person thinks if he feels strongly about where a "Black man's" place is in today's society.

Having a black man in the highest position in the country in something that was way beyond any ones expectation, especially white folks. I'm sure they never thought in a million years that the unpredictable would ever happen. However; we as black folks have always had the idea dancing around in our heads that it could possibly happen one day, and now the impossible was made into reality on Nov. 3, 2008. I'm - still pinching myself to see if I'm awake, and that this is not a dream. However; this was the dream that Dr. Martin Luther King Jr. had, and his dream came true.

These are the facts that we have to bring forth to our young people. We must teach them that dreams, no matter how small, or minute it may seen, can and will come true if it is intended to be a reality. It seems that lately the only reality that our young people are living is money, power, and death. They make the money selling their drugs, which gives them power, and they end up dead trying to hold on to those two demons. The demons becomes the master, and they becomes the servant. In any case they are imprisoned in their own cycle of madness, and it happens over, and over again. However; it is not too late to help them, even King Kong could be tamed to a certain point. But, these are children, not animals, so instead of trying to tame them lets try and train them, teach them, and love them as God loves us.

CHAPTER 4

The Change

What is change? In what way do we define the word "change". Is it a look? a thought? or an idea that can change our complete outlook on life? However; any decision that we make in life can change any circumstance that we're in at the time. A change can be temporary, or permanent depending on your lifestyle. Change should be for the better in all walks of life. While on the subject of life, the lives of so many children, babies, and adults alike are being drastically changed around the world with all the killing, and the drugs that has inhabited the lives of so many. The change that has happened from one decade to the other has changed all of our lives tremendously. It has corrupted so many young men lives. It seem to have given them this extra boost of power, nerves, and hearts of stone. They have no remorse for the sheer act of murder that they are committing daily. The world has gone all wrong. It seems to be completely of off it's axel, spinning out of control. Maybe that's why everything that is happening around us makes time seem to be moving like the matrix, in slow motion.

The change that came into Jeneen's life all those years ago, were good changes, a blessed change, as a matter of fact it was the best change that could have ever happen for Jeneen, and she has been making positive changes ever since. When our new president Barrack Obama started his campaign, his slogan was "time for a change." At that time he was just presenting a slogan that would make the world stand up and take notice, and realize that it really is a time for a change. Well it must have worked, because he is now president of the United States. The first black president to be exact.

Thinking back, I'm sure the race for president was not the only change the president was concerned about. The fact of the matter is' he was concerned about change around the world, in every aspect of life. Such as the economy, the school system, the children, and their parents, drugs, all the crimes that's being committed, and all other issues concerning a world change."

Just recently Janeen read a poster with a picture of Dr. Martin L. King on the top which said "I have a dream." And there was a picture of President Barrack Obama on the bottom which said "I am the dream." After reading that, she realize that there are a lot of possibilities that could still come from Dr. Kings dream, and from the dream that president Obama made into a reality. There is still hope that our young people will take notes from our positive leaders and would want to follow suite.

While Janeen gazed upon the face of Dr. King on the poster, her eyes looked from King to Obama, back and forth, comparing the features of two of the most important black men that she has ever known. The more she looked at Dr. King the more she could hear his words of the "I have a dream speech," and the words from some of his sermons. Although; she couldn't remember the words, she knew she loved listening to him talk. Now, here is President Obama, with the use of words just as powerful as Dr. King, which has drawn the attention of the entire world. We can only hope that the dreams he has will bring forth the change the world needs today.

An effort is being made with groups around the country giving what they call a "city year," as advertised on television. It's an organization of young people that gives a year of their time to helping other young people that's less fortunate. It's in some way similar to the big brother, and big sister program. Well, there are lots of young folks out there that really needs help. I'm now hoping that some one will start a program with the theme "think" in hopes that it will teach people to start thinking before doing something stupid, like killing someone because he didn't have any money in his pockets, or the person didn't want to give up what he worked so hard for, or because someone just walk away from them. Lately the young people around the world has been doing some really stupid things. With the world moving as fast as it is, we all need to set aside some time to do some serious mind blowing thinking. We need that slow deep involved thinking, the kind that will give us the opportunity to see where our thoughts will take us. With out sounding redundant, I'm sure our President "Barrack Obama" gave a lot of thought to the possibility of running for President, and while he campaigned, he gave a lot of thought to what he would do once he became president, and I'm sure each thought was carefully thought out from the first idea of ever becoming a politician. He is a perfect example of some one that thinks before he react, or speaks.

CHAPTER 5

War in Iraq and War in the Streets

In what way do we as a nation define the word "War." We may describe it as simple as a fight between enemies. Well! That is not much different from the dictionary version of war. It says "War is a state, or a period of open and declared armed fighting between states and nations of enemies; It's also a state of hostility, conflict, or antagonism, and struggle between opposing forces." Now if we all just step back, and take a good look at our surroundings in the neighborhood, read the news paper, or look at the nightly news, it is a perfect description of what a war is. The very thing that is happening in Iraq is also happening right here in our streets everyday. We are fighting a war just to stay alive, and to keep our children alive.

How do we deal with the trauma of a simple holiday for children like Halloween turns deadly? How are we to know what goes through the mind of raving lunatic who thinks the sound of children trick or treating is the sound of someone coming to rob him, and he opens fire killing a young boy, and wounding his brother and his father. That definitely sounds like war; "shoot first and ask questions later." which seems to be the way people around the world are handling their disputes these days.

Going back to the Halloween shooting; after looking at that young man's picture on the news, it is not hard to imagine that his imagination just ran away with him. And now that he has that kind of character, he has created all kinds of trouble for himself. Not to mention what he has done that family. Now every Halloween they have to rewind, and remember the senseless murder of their child. That is not the only act of killing some one without thinking, there is the unthinkable stabbing for a Little Debbie cake, or the shooting of a sister, or brother for as little as ten, or fifteen dollars. There is also the friend killing a friend with a garden rake. These are just a few of the war like activities that is going on in the streets. There are countless others, and not only in this town but in every town, city and state around the world.

There could be war raging in the minds of the most common looking folks. Some one that you least expect to do something stupid like shoot a police officer, when his only crime was doing his job, stopping speed demons. The streets are running red with the blood of so many people young and old, when a friend, family member, or just an enemy decides to strike out by stabbing, beating, or doing a drive by. There's an old saying "keep your friends close, and your enemies closer." I guess when that cliché was thought of, little did some people know that that would mean keeping their brother closer, because, in some cases, the brother was the enemy.

I guess it's not hard to imagine life in prison after hearing of some of the crimes that's being committed out here in the streets, I'm sure when those folks get together in prison, I can only imagine the different war stories they tell to each other. Who knows they may even have the opportunity to demonstrate a little of what they can do on some other poor sap that's in jail for a shorter time, or a lesser crime then theirs. There's some that has nothing to lose because they've got life. So what's it to them to stomp another mans head into the concrete. "What the heck, if I'm gonna die I might as well take some one with me." We may be oblivious to the fact that the war in Iraq has spilled into our streets, and from the streets to the prisons, but it is something going on that's causing us to lose our young people by the drove. Things are happening so fast it's frightening. It dose not seem real. What the world need the most of right now is prayers, lots and lots of prayers for every thing, and everybody around the world.

CHAPTER 6

"Please Help me! I don't want to die"

When we wake up in the mornings it's by the grace of God, then we look around, and thank God for our life and our family's life. We then ask God to help us to make a difference by "changing the things that we can, and accepting those things that we can not change". That is a daily prayer that we all can live by. One thing Janeen has asked God to help her to change, is the lives of our young folks. While walking around in the mall or, just walking past a young man on the street, try looking into his eyes, try your best to look beyond the over sized pants, the shirt that's five sizes too big, or the tough facial expressions. Look as closely as possible in their eyes, you will see sadness, and a cry for help. They're saying "save me before I die." Even though they try to keep the tough guy persona, it is actually just a front so that they wouldn't look like a "punk" to the other guys. These young people really do want to be saved.

As we look around at the young men and women we realize that the strongest influences in our young people's lives is money, clothes, cars and being some ones baby daddy. It is not about family anymore. A force stronger that a family's bond has finally come into our universe and separated the only natural thing that man based its existence on, "the family bond." We were brought up to believe that the family that "prays together stays together." There were even pictures of President Kennedy, and Dr. Martin Luther King Jr. and their families kneeling down for prayer, and I believe that families around the world began doing the same thing in hopes that prayer will keep their families together.

I wonder, (*perhaps along with many other families*), if taking prayers out of the schools was the right thing to do. Even as a child many years ago I remember how much I looked forward to saying the "*morning prayer*" and the "*pledge of allegiance*" when we got to school. It's no wonder our children are having such a hard time staying in school. They are constantly being confronted by Satan. When prayers were taken out of school, Satan stepped in, and all we can do is set back and let it continue. And our children has been falling by the way side ever since. For the most part they act as though they are possessed with a demonic spirit, and when the spirit gives them a task they can not resist the temptation. To them every thing evil looks good, and they must be a part of it.

However; if there was a way for us to separate one child at a time from his "homeboys," showing him a different way of life, and giving him the opportunity to change his life, we could have him believe that if he does not make a change "he will die." We must do this! Even if it has to be with one child at a time. "*Proverbs* 14:16"-A wise man fears and departs from evil; but the foolish rages on feeling confident." So let us teach these young people that it is better to fear, rather than to rage on not knowing if death is a close proximity to them.

I often wonder what goes through the mind of a person man, woman, or child when they shoot, stab, or beat someone to death. Do they feel any remorse, or sorrow for what they do. Most will say I'm sorry to the family while in court; But are they really sorry for what they do or sorry that they got caught? I guess we will never know would we! In some cases there is a chance that a person may kill someone in self- defense, but self defense is when you hit a person once just to get them of off you. However; when you hit a person repeatedly after they are down, then you are committing an act of "murder." I'm not writing this for those that know and understand that. I'm writing this for those young men that stands before a Judge in a court room and say "I killed him or her in self defense after they've shot some one three or four times, or to bludgeon someone to death you have to hit them more than two or three times,." that is not self defense, it is out right murder, which is not a misdemeanor, it is mandatory hard time. For some reason, that concept is not registering in these young folks head.

Some how, we have to start trying to save these young men and women. I've suggested one child at a time. But, in the mean time, people are still being killed for little or no reason, and it's getting worse. Perhaps the young people are trying to make a name for them selves so that they will be remembered. *Psalm* 6: *Verse* 5: reads "For in death there is no remembrance of thee: in the grave who shall give thee thanks?" Therefore; we have to come up with a master plan to keep our children out of the graves, and the sooner the better.

The last eleven years has brought the world a lot of tragedies starting with the 911/2001 World Trade Center disaster, Hurricane Katrina, the great tsunami in Indonesia, the fires in California, the killing of so many children, the death of Michael Jackson, Farrah Fawcett, Ed Mcman, and last but not least, the earth quake in Haiti

that has claimed the lives of at least one hundred thousand people. There are many more disasters that have taken place within the last eleven years, it's hard to remember them all. The year 2009 will not be an easy year to forget. However; we can make 2010 an even better year to put into our collection of memorable years, starting with putting more time and energy in saving our youths. We need to do whatever we can, as soon as we can, to save them. Because, everyday, even though we may not hear them, they are crying out for our help. These children really don't want to die they want to live, even if we have to save them from themselves.

CHAPTER 7

Love of a child

From the first day of birth, the day your child enters this world, there is a love every mother feels that's like no other. It's more love than the love for your husband, your mother, your father, sister, or brother. It is an inspiration beyond words. It's a stimulant that makes your heart beat fast, and slow at the same time. It can be a breath taking emotion that brings tears to your eyes. But, they're tears of joy and happiness. The fact that you can bring one of Gods greatest gifts into this cruel world is proof that God wants you to be a mother or a father. Now with all of that in mind, how can we as parents do such awful, despicable things to our children? How can any one look into the eyes of a baby or a little child and say mom and dad loves you so very much, and then an hour later you're slapping then beside the head so hard it takes their breath away, or perhaps you shake them so vigorous it stops their heart, and you just walk away.

I've often wondered if a mother looks into her child's eyes just before putting him or her into the microwave oven, or tossing it out of a moving car window, leaving them buckled into their car seats and letting it roll into the lake. I realize that as adults we are faced with a lot of stress within our homes, our work places, in our relationships with our spouse, and in most cases with our children. But there are support groups for that, such as counselors, psychologists, priests, pastors or just church members to talk to before we make a horrible mistake and do something that we will regret, and have to live with for the rest of our lives.

Every one knows that the eyes are the window to the souls, and even though a child is "A child" they also have feelings and a soul. Maybe that would be the reason for not looking into their eyes when you give them a deadly mixture to drink, or you make sure they're sound to sleep before you get up the nerve to shoot, or stave them to death. I'm the mother of four children, who are all grown up now, but they were babies at one time and I went through all the stress, walking the floor at night, middle of the night feedings, the diaper changes, the period of cutting teeth, and all the other changes that babies go through as they're growing up, but none of those changes ever gave the thought of ever wanting to end one of their lives. With that being said, I wonder why some mothers find it so easy to kill their child, or children.

I can not help but wonder if those were "Spur of the moment decisions", or were the ideas dancing around in their heads for a while before doing the actual act. In any case murder is the most horrible act any parent can inflict upon a child. Children are a spin off of their parents. The way we think, or act, everything we do in front of our children is an easy way for them to mimic us. When we smoke, drink, or use profanity in their presence, it is almost for certain that they will do the same thing. I'm not saying a parent is not to do certain things to relax themselves, I'm just saying it's not good to do it in front of your child. Janeen smoked cigarettes, drank beer, and smoked pot, (years ago of course), but to this day her children will tell any one that they never saw her do it in their presence. My point is, if we respect ourselves, and our children, they will intern respect us. It is time for us to love our children more, and the ways of the world less. Let's face it the world is consuming our children. It is literally destroying their lives bit by bit. It would be a miracle if there's enough young men left to start another generation within the next twenty years or so. If someone is not killing them, then, they're killing themselves, or each other. It is time for the madness to end. It is time to show a child that there is nothing more important in your life than the love you have for him or her. Show God the love you possess in your heart for a child.

CHAPTER 8

"Help us to understand about Jesus"

"Fiction"

The moral of this story "Help us to understand about Jesus" is about a group of young people, boys and girls. Some are good, and some are bad, but they are all standing at the cross roads in their lives trying to decide which way they want to go. They've seen so much death of family and friends. However; there is a community center right next to a church just waiting to help them, no matter what they decides to do. There is always some one at the center for the kids to talk to, games for them to play, and it even has a library.

The community is a haven for all sorts of kids, because it's in an all black area "the hood" that's in the middle of down town. It is surrounded by everything, all sorts of gangs, pool halls, and clubs. There are always shootings, murders, and drug dealings going on, and it surrounds the center. There is a care taker who is at the center when no one knows he's there, and he sees all, and hears all, but he's too afraid to go to the police with any of it. He's also afraid of retaliation from the hood rats, so he just keeps his mouth shut. The Pastor, and other community leaders are trying hard to change things in the community with the young people. They realize that it will take people coming together, and the love of God in their hearts to set things in order. Their work is certainly cut out for them.

Characters:

Pastor: George White- pastor of The Church of Christ United- and head of The Community Center.

Sister: Rosa Smith-Asst. at Community Center.

Sister: Rita Major- Associate Pastor.

Sister: Mary Jones- Church busy body.

Brother/Deacon: Malcom Montgomery- In charge of hiring people for the center.

Sister: Marie Brown- Community Center Counselor.

Sisters: Sally Reese, Cynthia Maple, Janet Wright- leaders for young girls.

Brothers: Richard Richardson, Robert Young, James Peoples- leaders for young boys.

Troubled Youths: Shanea Tindal, Rochine Powel, Anthony Tindal, (Shanea's brother), Quinaza(hot papa) Jones, Sara Young.

Drug dealers: Frank(dollar bill)Taylor, Tyreak(Mr. T)Forman, Simon(S.K.) King, Rodney(R.J.)Jamerson.

Good Kids: Sarah Mobley, Martin Malone, Synara Perks, Frank King Jr.(older brother to Simon King), Ramond Rogers, Francis Scars.

Simon Rogers: community care taker (father to Raymond Rogers).

The Play: Time settings: Sunday Morning- Sunday Morning of the following weekend:

Pastor White: It is good to see you all at church this Sunday morning, especially my young people!

Congregation: Praise the Lord Reverend!

Narrator: The Pastor preached his sermon, and at the end he announced that during the past week he was also at the community center for any youth that needed to talk about anything.

Sister: Rita Jones-Associate Pastor- It is with profound sadness to announce the killing of another one of our youths. He was shot to death last Saturday night at a club just around the corner from the center. So please young people, if there's anything bothering you please come to the center and talk to us.

Congregation: Amen Sister Rita.

Narrator: Church service ends and folks stands around talking about meeting at the center on Monday evening.

Monday evening: Sister Rosa Smith, (night manager at the center) was sitting at her desk when some young folks walks in. It was Shanea Tindal, and her brother Anthony Tindal.

Shanea: I heard in the wind that you folks can help people like me, and my brother. So tell me in what way can you help us? You gonna give us some money, a home, our parents back? So how can you help us?

Anthony: Yea! What can you do for us? I can use a new pair of Nikes, they cost about $ 95.00, can you do that for me?

Sister Rosa Smith: Hello! I'm Sis. Smith. What are your names? I'm Shanea, and this is my brother, Anthony.

Sis. Smith: I want to welcome you both to the center. What we do here at the center is, we try to communicate with our youth through counseling, and then we see what we can do to help, where help is needed.

Shanea: I don't need to talk, what I need is money!

Anthony: Me too, so what's up old lady?

Narrator: At that same moment, Pastor White walked in and introduced himself as Pastor of the Church of Christ United across the street, and the director of this community center.

Pastor White: Is there something I can do for you young folks, besides the money you're asking for, because we don't keep money here. We can give you a meal, some conversation if that will help.

Shenea: We can talk to each other, if we wanted to talk; as a matter of fact we have more people to talk to. Here are our friends Rochine, Quinaza, but we call him (hot papa), and this young lady is my girl Sara.

Anthony: So you see, if we wanted to carry on a conversation old man, we got plenty of people to talk too.

Narrator: About thirty minutes later Sis. Prescott, and Bro. Richardson walked in, (who are both choir directors) singing along with the youth choir members which sings for the community center.

Sis. Prescott: Good evening Sis. Smith, Pastor White. So what do we have here, some new members for our youth choir.

Sis. Smith: No! Sis. Prescott, I'm afraid these young people are not looking for any choir to sing on, they're looking for trouble, but what they need is prayer.

Bro. Richardson: Well we got plenty of that to give out, cause we all need prayer, especially our young folks.

Bro. Simon Rogers: The community center care taker, who also joined in the conversation, adding that, "these young folks also needs a good whipping, and some guidance. I see what be going on out there in them streets day and night. There is always some kid getting beat up and left for dead, or just plain getting shot to death. I know a lot more about what's going on out there than you kids think I know".

Sis. Mary Jones: Well I've heard everything, I got to call Sis, Inez and tell her what she missed by not being at the center tonight. Ring!!! Hello!! Hello, is this Sis Inez,

Inez: Yes, Speaking!

Sis Mary Jones: This Mary, Mary Jones, Girl I just had to call you and tell you what you missed at the center tonight.

Sis Inez: How do you do Mary! So what did I miss at the center tonight?

Sis. Mary Jones: Well, some hoodlums, and some drug dealers came into the center, I I really think they came with the intentions of robbing the place, but, after Pastor White, and Pastor Major talked to them for a while, I think they changed their minds and then they left. I got a feeling they might be at church on Sunday.

Inez: Well it would be a blessing if they would come to church. Maybe some others will follow them.

Mary Jones: Well let's pray that they do come, cause they really needs to be saved. Well any way I'll see you on Sunday Sis Inez.

Inez: Yes! Sis Mary, you have a blessed night.

Narrator: The rest of the week passed and there was not any other incidents at the Center, as a matter of fact things seemed rather quiet. On Sunday morning at the Church of Christ United, Sunday school started on time as usual, and nothing seemed different until seven or eight young people began strolling in one at a time. It was a sight to behold to see all those young people wanting to change their lives. It seems that what was said to them at the center must have taken root, because here they are.

Pastor George White: Praise the Lord everybody, we have a lot to praise God for this day. It is a blessing to see so many young people visiting with us today. Sometimes we feel that our words befall deaf ears, but we know that God is in charge of everything. Let us all stand and welcome our young visitors, and if they would like to say something now is the time.

Frank Taylor (dollarbill): When we left the center the other night, (and I'm speaking for everyone with me) we discussed what we heard, and thought a lot about what we heard, and we realized that it is time that we try living on the other side of the fence for a change. I am, and I'm sure I speak for everyone else when I say that we are tired of the sickness in the street, and we want you all to help us to understand about Jesus, and how he can change our lives.

Rita Major(asst. pastor) Praise the Lord, well you have come to the right place. This is where it all begins, and you've got to start somewhere. Church let's all stand and greet these young folks. Shake their hands, hug them, or do whatever God lays on your heart, let's just make them feel welcome.

Pastor white: Choir! sing a song that will bring the power of the lord in this church house Today----Amen! Narrator------ As the choir began to sing the entire church burst into a frenzy of joyous Shouts of Hallaluah! And praise the Lord! As the spirit of the Lord came in the church house. When the shouts settled down there was tears of joy in the eyes of those young people. Even though this is just a fictional play, with fictional characters, it is just an idea of how the lives of some of your peers are in the real world. "If you learn to live, you will learn to love."

CHAPTER 9

"Wake Up"

"Fiction"

"Wake up is a fictional story about two guys "best friends" that leaves a small town, and moves to a bigger city "New York" which was the mistake of a life time".

Characters: Walter, Fred and Ray, who everyone calls the "gunman".

"Man we finally made it to the big city, and today is such a beautiful day, I wonder what we can get into today" said Walter as he looked out over the balcony of the high rise apartment that he shares with his best friend "Fred" in New York City.

"What do you mean when you say "get into today, Walt? Do you mean get into, as in girls or trouble"? asked Fred.

Walter chuckled and said "man you know that getting with the girls can also mean trouble, with a capital "T" if you know what I mean!

"Yea man, I know what you mean", said Fred, at least where the ladies are concerned, but what do you mean get in today?

"Fred!!!" Said Walter, looking back at him with a look of confusion on his face, as if wondering" why is Fred acting as if he really didn't know what he meant?, and Fred looking back at Walter with the same confused look.

"Damn man"! said Walter, look around you, look down there. There is so much money to be made here. This is New York, not that little small hick town we came from in South Carolina.

"Yeah man" said Fred, but the small stuff we did there didn't amount to much, and we were able to hit it and quit it.

"Yeah! It was small alright" yelled Walter" with a smirk on his face. Small drugs, small money, small minded people, and all the small stuff was the reason we left that small town in the first place.

"So tell me man what do you have in mind? Ask Fred, as he watched his friend walk from one end of the balcony to the other, as if he was doing some heavy thinking and planning at the same time.

Well, to begin with we need to see how much money we have, "Said Walter", and then we need to find the happening spots.

As the two men readied themselves to leave their apartment, the thought hit them both at the same time, but Fred said it first "man what if we don't have enough money to do anything with?"

Then Walter said "man you know I thought the same thing, but if we don't, we'll have to get it somehow.

"So you know somebody here we can go to? Ask Fred!

"HELL NO" shouted Walter, but we will get to know somebody real fast."

They walked out the door feeling o.k. about the decisions they've just made. "As I see it, someone may be in trouble," said Walter.

When they got to the bank, they discovered that there was only 150.00 dollars, and that was not nearly enough for what they had in mind. When Walter and Fred walked out of the bank, Walter was so angry he hit the wall of the bank with his fist.

"Damn it" said Walter, I really thought we had more money than this in there, I guess we just have to go to plan "B".

What's plan "B" asked Fred?

"Plan "B", said Walter, may cause somebody to get hurt, namely us if anything goes wrong.

"What do you mean "if anything goes wrong? Ask Fred. What are we going to do, rob a bank? grinning at the same time, and trying not to sound serious at all.

Then, Walter turned to look at Fred with a "chessor cat' grin on his face. "The first thing we need to do is see where we can buy us a couple of guns with this 150.00 dollars," said Walter.

"GUNS" shouted Fred, no man not guns, what you really need to do is WAKE UP from that dream you're having, because the only place guns will get us is locked up or killed.

"Yeah man! You might be right" Walter said, in a sarcastic tone, but it can also get us rich, if we play our cards right!

The two friends walked away from the bank with the crazy notion of looking for some place to buy a gun, or someone to show them where to go. They walked from place to place until they came upon a guy selling boot-leg stuff from the trunk of his car.

"Hey man what's up" said Walter. They call me Walt, and this is my friend Fred. "Say man what do they call you? Ask Fred

They call me the "Gun Man", but my name is Ray.

"Well Ray, Someone told us that you might give us a good deal on some guns," said Walter, (as his eyes darted from side to side)

"That depends on how much you're willing to spend," said the gunman.

"Well man what can 150.00 dollars get me? Cause that's all I got! said Walt.

"Yeah man that's all we got! followed Fred.

"All you got ha? Ask the gunman. What about that watch? With the watch and the 150.00 you can get two guns.

Walter looked back at Fred as if to ask if he should do it. Fred hunched his shoulders as if to say "man it's up to you." Walter turned back to the gunman and agreed to the watch and 150.00. The man put the guns in a brown paper bag like they just bought milk and bread. Here you go man, just don't tell anyone where you got them from! Said the gunman. "That's a bet man" said Walt, and he and Fred walked away feeling as if they've just made the deal of their lives. Not really thinking about what their next move is going to be, at least not without a plan.

"Now what man? Asked Fred.

Well! We are going to take these guns and make us some money! Said Walt. There's a bank on every block. We can take it, either just after it opens, or just before it closes.

What do you think Fred? Asked Walter.

Fred "looking at Walter as if to say, man you're crazy, but I'm going along with your crazy idea this time, I think just before closing would be a better time because it's less people, it's also almost dark.

Yeah man! you're right, that's the best idea you've had yet, now we have a plan, said Walt.

The two men had a few hours before the bank started closing, so they walked from block to block checking out all the banks. As they walked, they couldn't help but notice all the huge buildings, and all the people walking the streets.

"This should be a piece of cake," said Walt.

"What do you mean" ask Fred

Well! Once we do the stick and get the money we can get lost in this crowd of people, and stick with them until we get back to our hotel; announced Walt.

"Sounds easy enough"! Said Fred.

But little did they know that it wasn't as easy as it sound, to begin with they didn't figure the bank would have a security guard, or the bank having a silent alarm. Their plan was set in motion at 4:45 pm when they stormed in the bank, guns a blazing, shooting into the ceiling, and then into the floor, as if trying hard not to shoot others, or one another. That went on for about 20 minutes, then all of a sudden, police officers was coming from every direction, their guns also blazing. The first to get shot was Fred, he was shot in the leg, and then Walt was shot in the arm. I guess the police didn't want them dead, but just wounded enough for them to go to jail. They were both taken to the Hospital. Fred was admitted because the area where he was shot in the leg was a major artery, and it was life threatening. Walt wound, however, was not so bad, therefore; he was treated and released, and was taken straight to jail.

Sometime had passed, and both men went to court. Walt was given 15 years in prison without parole. Fred was also given 15 years in prison, but he was still very ill, and the majority of his time was spent in the hospital part of the prison, because he was in jeopardy of losing his right leg. Once he was stable enough, through the dizziness, and grogginess Fred manage to ask about his friend Walt. He wanted to know where he was. The nurses all looked at each other, and one finally said "your friend is in prison, and so are you.

'Well! I knew this would happen "Said Fred", I tried to talk him out of it, but he wouldn't listen to me, now look at us, we're prisoners, and I may lose my leg.

Several months passed, and Fred got well enough to leave the hospital and was able to go to the population part of the prison, in a wheel chair of course. Again; weeks passed, and Fred finally got to see his friend Walt.

"Hey Fred my man" said Walt, how you doing man? Damn it's good to see you!"

"I'm ok man", said Fred! Just trying to get used to this wheel chair, well; I guess it will take some time, since time is all I've got now, and the doctor said I'll probably never walk again".

"That is some mess up stuff man, and I'm real sorry about that Fred, said Walt." I should have listen to you man, you tried to tell me this would happen.

"I did try to tell you, Didn't I"! Said Fred.

They both laughed as if what they did was as minor as "stealing cookies out of a cookie jar. But as quickly as the smiles came, it also disappeared, as if they finally realized that they were headed for a long, hard stay in prison. The time came for the two friends to go to their cells. Fred's cell was on the first floor because of his wheel chair, but Walt was on the second floor.

A couple of years passed, and both Fred and Walt settle in and started thinking on the straight and narrow. They started attending the church services on Sunday, reading the Bible, and going to Bible study. They were both trying to become model prisoners.

However; there was this one prisoner that was serving life, (*and had nothing to lose*) felt as though he owned some of the prisoners. One particular day while the prisoners were on the yard, Walt was reading his Bible, and for some reason this guy did not like him reading it. He preceded to take it from Walt, and of course, Walt fought back, and he was stabbed with a homemade shank. He died shortly after that, but before he died, he asked the guard to give Fred a message for him. He said, "Tell Fred he was right when he said that we could end up in jail, dead, or both. Tell him he was a good friend, and I'm sorry I did not listen to him. THE END

This short story (Wake Up) is just a short explanation as to how quickly any one can get pulled into a situation that may cause them their life. If any

young person feel that any ideas your friends may have, and you don't think it's quite right according to your standard, don't go along with him because he's your friend, you just may become a victim of your friends idea for trouble. Do the opposite try and talk him out of it, and if that does not work, then, go tell someone else that may have a little more influence on your friend. Try to do everything you could possibly do to sway his mind, if there is nothing left after that, then, you need to go your separate ways, or have regret as Walt did in the end.

"Basic Black"

Murdered Spirits Unrest

These fiction stories are about all the black people that were killed somehow by Police Officers in one way or another, or by vigilantes. However; only a few or none of the officers was charged for the crimes. The public and families were told that the officers were within their rights when the victim/victims were murdered. That may have been a final decision as far as the Chief of Police, the court or anyone else who made the decision to not punish those officers. " which was a mistake". The officers committed the crimes of killing someone that was unarmed, or who had not done anything that warranted death. These officers will realize that they made the wrong decision. It does not matter how anyone view the shootings/killings, it all boils down to the fact that they all committed murder. As times passed each of the officers started

seeing the person they killed in different visions. Each victim appeared to their killer multiple times, It got so bad, to the point of them seeing a Doctor, and then a Shrink. But, little did they know, they will need more than a shrink to stop the demise that would soon befall them. One at a time every Police Officer or any one that took the life of an innocent person will eventually meet their fate. These Unrest Murdered Spirits and the stories of how their lives ended is fiction, so is the fate of the people that murdered them is fiction. These murdered spirits cannot fine peace in their death until they feel Justice have been served, and each person have been punished for their crimes. Only this time the officers would be the victims, and the Dead will inflict the punishment.

By: Joan J. Davis

Story 1

This story began August 24, 1955 in Jackson MS. when Emmanuel Thomas a young black 14 year old boy was beaten and tortured to death by two white men all because he touched the hand of a white cashier. Emmanuel Thomas crime was not flirting with a white girl. His true crime was being black, and flirting with a white girl. Both men were acquitted for the crime. They may have been found not guilty by a court of their peers, and thought they got away with murder, but the spirit of Emmanuel Thomas had other ideas of how to make them pay for what they did to him. A little time passed and everything seemed calm to Ray Brown, and J.B Miller, the two men that murdered Emmanuel Thomas. But, little did they know that their time was winding down. The first vision appeared before Ray Brown while he was sitting on his front porch. Emmanuel appeared first normal, the way he looked before they killed him. Ray freaked out, jumped up and ran to his truck, looking back to see if Thomas was still after him. He cranked his truck, started down the road, and yelling J. B. Miller's name as he drove fast and looking back at the same time. Just as he turn to look in front Emmanuel Thomas appeared before him again, only this time he was beaten, swollen, and looked exactly the way he looked when they took him out of the water. When Ray Brown saw that vision he lost control of his truck. It started to flip and he ended up in a trench of the side off the road. He was dead on impact. But it didn't stop there. Once Emmanuel realized that Ray was out of the way, he turned his focused in on J.B. Miller.

Emmanuel appeared to J.B. Miller while he was sitting on the toilet in his out house. Although it was dark in the outhouse and the only light was a small candle burning on a small wooden shelf. As we all know a candle gives of flickering images, which makes you see things that aren't really there. Well, that image became real for J.B. Miller, because the vision that appeared before him was so frightening, he couldn't believe his eyes. Emmanuel Thomas appeared in his beaten and battered look. Even the bullet hole glowed from the flickering light. All Miller could say over, and over again was, you're dead, you're dead, we killed you. But, the spirit of Emmanuel Thomas just kept steering at him until he jumped of off the toilet and started running toward his house, but before he could reach the door, he fell and died right there. The coroner said it was a heart attack. He died with his eyes wide open as if he was frightened to death. Little did they know it was the spirit of Emmanuel Thomas that caused his demise. From that point on, there were Police Officers and vigilantes dying all over the place. That's because none or most of them have not been punished for the murders they committed. Well; these unrest murdered spirits will see to it that they get just what they deserve.

REST IN PEACE EMMANUEL

Story2

Shortly after Tyrone Moten was murdered by Gary Lieberman on Feb. 26, 2012 for absolutely no reason, Lieberman's life began to change. He started to feel a sense of panic within him, especially after the court decided not charge him with Moten's murder. He found himself awaken many nights from nightmares, cold sweats, and panting for breath. He had not had a good night sleep since the murder. He started drinking just to drown his thoughts. Perhaps his thoughts were about "why he took the life of such a young boy. With his only excuse being "he feared for his life, with the stand your ground law." The only weapon Tyrone had was a drink, candy and his cell phone. However; the fact that Lieberman was not punished for his crime, the spirit of Tyrone Moten will see to it he gets what he deserves. The first appearance Moten made to Lieberman was about a year later when Lieberman was in one of his drunken hangovers. He stepped outside to get some fresh air, just as he looked up he saw Moten, cladded in the same black hoodie he had on that night, and he was looking straight at him. Lieberman blinked his eyes several times to make sure of what he just saw, and if it was real. Yes it was real, and he would soon find out just how real it was. Moten let a day past, and Lieberman thought that what he saw was just a figment of his imagination, and went on about his life as normal. However; just as he got comfortable in his skin, Tyrone made another appearance to him. This time it was in broad daylight. Tyrone was sitting in the passenger seat of Lieberman's car. When Lieberman saw him he almost ran off the road, he looked again and the image was gone. At that point he thought he was losing his mind. He started wondering "why was he seeing images of Tyrone Moten" he knew Moten was dead, but why was his mind playing tricks on him? He did not understand what was going on. Once he got home, he started playing around with his guns. After he cleaned them, every once in a while he would play a little Russian roulette by himself. A few times he would put the gun to his head, and pull the trigger. Each time it just clicked. The third time he put the gun to his head, the Spirit of Tyrone Moten appeared before him. He didn't realize there was a bullet left in the barrel, and when he pulled the trigger this time the gun fired, and he was killed by his own self infliction.

At that moment the spirit of Tyrone Moten faded away, as if he could finally rest in peace after justice had been served. When the Police and the Coroner arrived, it looked as though Lieberman had committed suicide. As far as the Police was concerned the case was closed. However; they did ask questions around town to see if Lieberman had been acting a little strange. Some people said he acted as though something was bothering him. Then he made the statement to several people "I know that nigger is dead, I know he is dead" so why do I keep seeing him. No one answered him, because they didn't understand what he was talking about. After hearing those answers, the Police determined that Lieberman killed himself. Perhaps he felt guilty for the death of Tyrone Moten, and gave himself the death sentence. But, it didn't stop there, the officers and other people that's guilty of killing someone for little or no reason started dying. They were popping up dead all over, everywhere. Even if the offender was found guilty of murder and put in jail, it was not easy to hide from the unrest spirit of the dead. Rest in Peace Tyrone Moten.

Story 3

Jimmy Daniels was the next unfortunate 17 year old that was murdered on Nov. 27,2012 by Marvin Dinkins because of loud noises coming from a truck that parked next to him. It was a senseless murder that made headlines around the world. Even though Dinkins was arrested and charged with murder, he still was not safe from Jimmy Daniel's unrest spirit. About a month after Dinkins was put in jail, he started feeling as though he was being watched, not by the Prison Security, but by something he could not see. He even mentioned it, first to his cellmate, and later to the Security. They actually told him that he was starting to lose his mind, or he was just feeling the pressure of being locked up. He may have been satisfied with that answer if the feeling was not so strange. He actually felt that someone was riding on his back, with legs straddled around his neck. This is when he's up and walking around during the day, at night it felt like someone was straddling his chest as he laid in bed. The weight was so heavy he could barely breathe or turn over in his bed. The attack of the spirit of Jimmy Daniels upon Marvin Dinkins went on for quite a long time, to the point of having Dinkins see a doctor, a specialist to be exact. He explained to the doctor what he was experiencing. The doctor performed a few simple tests which lead him to tell Dinkins "there was nothing physically wrong with him," and judging from what Dinkins told him he realized that Dinkins was being haunted by a spirit. The Doctor said it was a very powerful spirit, and he needed to see an exorcist. However; the fact that he was in jail for murder made it real hard to schedule an exorcist to perform an exorcism on him. As time went on the unrest spirit haunted Dinkins for so long it actually drove him insane. Once Jimmy Daniels task was done, and he realized that Dinkins was completely crazy to the point of not even knowing his own name. When he saw that Dinkins was a complete zombie, he was finally able to fade away to his final resting place. Rest in Peace Jimmy Daniels

Story 4

When Cedric Gains was murdered in Staten Island New York in 2014, it was not just one officer that was responsible for his death, it was several. Cedric was a big fellow, and it took all of the officers to bring him down. However; the one that held him in the chock hold was not charged with his death, the officer that was the blame was Sargent Missy Adams. Even though Cedric was a little out of shape, and a little on the heavy side, the Judge said that his unhealthy life style caused his death. Well he has no chance of improving that now. The question is "What did he do to deserve a death like that. As far as Cedric's unrest spirit is concern the officers that's responsible for his untimely demise will meet his spirit, and they will wish they never heard of Cedric Gains. The first person Cedric haunted was David Pinkney, the officer that put him in the chock hold, and held him like that until he stopped breathing. The time the officer came in contact with Cedric's unrest spirit was when he was out with his friends from the police department. There were only four of them at the table, but there were five chairs. When Officer Pinkney took a drink, and started laughing, he stopped in the middle of the laugh, and a look came over his face that was frightening to his friends. He actually saw Cedric sitting in the fifth chair. His friends asked him what was wrong. He said he thought he saw something, but it might have been his imagination. They jokingly told him that he needed to stop drinking. He just laughed it off, and continued to drink, but he couldn't stop thinking about what he thought he saw. He and his friends left the bar and each got into his own car and left. Officer Pinkney started driving toward home, and he looked in his rear view mirror, and saw Cedric Gains face again, but when he looked in the back seat, he didn't see anyone. At that moment a sense of fear rose up in Pinkney's mind. He didn't know what was going on. He just shook his head, as if to shake it off, and continued his drive home. He arrived home and told his wife what had been happening to him. She said it was just his mind playing tricks on him, and what he needs is a good night sleep. He agreed and began to get ready for bed. However; when he laid down, sleep was the last thing on his mind. He finally drifted off to sleep, but even in his sleep he saw Cedric Gains. Cedric was putting his arms around Pinkney's neck, it got tighter, and tighter until Pinkney could not breathe anymore. Pinkney died that night in his sleep. The coroner said it was like he just stopped breathing in his sleep. Cedric accomplished what he set out to do, "get even with one of the people responsible for his death Officer Pinkney was dead." However; Cedric was not finished yet, he had one more person to see before he could take his rest. Her name was Sargent Missy Adams. She was the officer that stood by while the other officer held Cedric in a choke hold, and did nothing about it. When Missy Adams saw what was happening to Cedric Gains it was her duty as Sargent in the department, to step up. Regardless of her being on duty, or just stopping by to see what was going on. She had the right to stop all of it. But the fact that she didn't is reason for her to be visited by the unrest spirit of Cedric Gains. Since she was stripped of her badge, and although she lost her title as Sargent, and put on desk duty is still not enough to keep her safe from Cedric Gains unrest spirit. The first encounter Missy had with the spirit of Cedric was while she sat at her desk at the Police Dept. She was doing some research for a case when all of a sudden a big black face appeared on her screen. She jumped back, startled and scared senseless as to what she had just seen. She blinked several times as to clear her eyes as she started looking at the screen again. Time passed, about a week, and Adams continued her search on the computer for a different case. This time it was about another black man that was shot and killed by a police officer. She leaned her head into her hands and began to sob a little. All of a sudden there was a voice in her head that said "at least he was shot, which was a quick death for him. But not for, me I was locked in a choke hold until I died. I suffered before I died." Missy Adams was confused as to what was going on in her head. She wondered why "all of a sudden" she started seeing Cedric Gains face everywhere, it was like she was being haunted. What Missy Adams didn't realize was that it was only the beginning of her demise.

When she left the Police Dept. that day and started for home, she decided to stop by the store to get a bottle of wine. She got home, made her something to eat, and poured her a glass of wine. She sat down to eat, while all the time thinking about the day she had had. She looked into her glass of wine. She saw his face and heard a voice saying "you let them kill me." She jumped up and poured the wine down the sink. She took a deep breath, gave a sigh and decided to get ready for bed. All the while wondering what was going on. Missy started to undress and all of a sudden a figure appeared in the mirror, the figure of a man, a big man. Just as she started to scream he reached through the mirror and caught her by the neck and began choking her, he did not stop until she was dead. Then as quickly as he appeared, he was also gone. He could finally rest in peace. When the Police found her it appeared as though she had a heart attack. The case was closed for Missy Adams and David Pinkney.

REST IN PEACE CEDRIC GAINS

Story 5

The suspicious deaths continued to happed, one after another. The next unrest spirit was that of Ronald Braxton, a 38 year old man killed in Arizona. He was shot and killed because an inhaler that was in his pocket appeared to be a weapon. Well, that's what was reported as the reason they shot and killed Braxton. The officer responsible for shooting Braxton is Mike Ramsey a seven year veteran in the department was not charged for the crime. Instead they took him off the street, and gave him a desk job. Ramsey (white by race) was never charged with murder. However; the fact that no one was charged for killing him, Braxton's unrest spirit will not stop until someone pays the price. Mike Ramsey continued to live his life as if he had done nothing wrong. He continued to hang out with his friends, family, etc. He had completely forgotten the fact that he had murdered an innocent man for having an inhaler that looked like a weapon in his pocket. Ramsey gave no apologies for what he had done to Braxton's family or anyone else for that matter. Well, now the haunting games begin. The first sighting Ramsey had of Braxton was when he was walking into work at the Police Station. There was a crowd of people walking around him. He looked over to his right and walking next to him was Ronald Braxton. Ramsey stood still in his tracks, frozen, as if he could not move, and just that fast the image was gone. He started looking around for another sighting, but there was none. Ramsey continued walking into the building. He got into the elevators and hit the button for the floor he wanted. After the elevator doors closed he could see a figure in the reflector doors. It looked a lot like the figure he saw earlier. He began to look around in the elevator to see if it was someone in there with him, but there was no one. He turned to look at the elevator doors again, and the figure was still there looking at him. The elevator finally stopped, Ramsey got off stumbling around, and talking to himself that he had seen a ghost in the elevator. He did that for a while, and his Captain finally told he had to see a Doctor, because he seemed to be having a nervous breakdown. He did see the doctor, and he was prescribed medication that should only be taken at night. However; Ramsey took the medication during the day, thinking it would stop him from having visions of Braxton in his head. But, little did he know that the medication was to help him to sleep at night, and not to be taken during the day. After taking two pills he decided to go for a drive, he began to get sleepy, as the sleep over powered him, he started to drift off. He ran off the right side of a bridge, and as he was tumbling the vision of Braxton's face stayed with him until he closed his eyes and died. At that moment Braxton's spirit was finally able to rest, after he saw to it that his killer was punished.

REST IN PEACE: RONALD BRAXTON

Story 6

There have been several different instances where they found people that died suddenly in strange ways, in different Cities. Well; this is another such incident. On one clear week day morning some of the officers were on their way to work at the New Iberia La. Police Station in La. One officer had an accident and ran off the side of a bridge, and crashed at the bottom, once the car stopped rolling, the spirit of Vince Ward got out of the car look over the bridge, smiled, and said "there's one down" and others to go, and he moved on to look for his next victim.

Everything was going good at the station. The officers were getting their reports together for the day, and talking about the accident of the other officer while he was on his way to work. They also mentioned how it seemed to have been a freak accident, because he didn't have a heart attack, or blacked out he just drove of off the bridge. Vince knew exactly what happened. Meanwhile; Vince Ward was looking around for the other Officers that he remembered arrested him that day. He knew it was several, but he didn't see all of their faces at the time of his arrest. However; being a spirit allowed him the ability to move among the people with ease. He finally spotted another one of the officers that arrested him, which was the one that shot me in the chest, causing my death, and lied to the Chief saying that I shot myself." I'm really going to enjoy hurting him. For a long while Vince just sat around and watched the officer all day until it was time for him to get off work. Once the Officer clocked out, and was off work for the day, Vince Ward knew just what he had in mind for the second officer responsible for his death. Vince followed the officer to his car, not the squad car, but his own personal vehicle. He actually got in the front seat beside the officer. He stared at him for a very long time. "I guess he was trying to figure out why this man wanted me dead?" Why did he shot me in the chest? and told everyone that I shot myself while I was handcuffed from behind. Vince pondered those thoughts for a moment, and decided, well; all that's water under the bridge. Now is my time to get even. Vince watched as the officer took out his revolver, looked at it, and laid it on the dash. He wondered what was going through the office's head. He looked over at the passenger side of his car, as if he could see Vince. But, we know that was impossible, because, Vince was a spirit, a ghost, he couldn't be seen. Well something must have happened to his mind at that moment, because within those seconds he had gotten the gun of off the dash and shot himself in the chest. It was a hole big enough to put a fist through. As a matter of fact, it was the same size wound that was in my chest they said I administered to myself. Well after Vince saw what the officer did to himself, he felt a since of satisfaction for what they had done to him, and now he can finally go to his resting place.

REST IN PEACE VINCE WARD.

Story 7

It is truly amazing to have been able to live your life Yavern, with your twin sister Yolanda. Someone that looks like you, dressed like you, and on certain occasions you could even play tricks on people, like a set of twin boys played on me and my sister when we were in school. They were identical. I've always wondered what it would be like if I had a twin sister, but no such luck, I ended up with just a plain old sister. I'm sure you used tohave fun with your twin sister, someone that was your best friend. When this officer, (who obviously did not have any experience in handling domestic disputes), fired upon Yolanda the second she answered her door, and ended her life in such a cruel and heartless way. And now, here you are, longing for the day you can just hug her again, and to tell her how much you love her.

You can't help but wonder what a man like deputy David Wells was doing on the force in Beastrop County, when he was turned down for the job in Trias County, they did not hire him. He also tried to get work at Astin police Department, and he also did not get hired there. Now the question is why is working at the Bastrop Sheriff Dept? It is not clear why he wanted to check out a domestic disturbance when he was not cleared to do so. To begin with he had no experience with domestic disputes, and the only thing he knew was to draw his gun and fire at the first person he came into contact with, which was Yolanda Stone. At the risk of sounding nostalgia, I know you wish you could turn back the hands of time. I know, I've been there, and done that. However; there is still a matter of finding out why was your sister Yolanda was killed, when her only crime was answering her front door. When some like you thinks about why certain events occurs in your life, the one thing you need to do is give it to the Lord and he will give you all the answers. The person that committed that horrible crime will get whatever is coming to him.

A little while after Yavern left the doctor's office that she was visiting, because she needed help adjusting to her sister's death. She was on her way to the Police station she witnessed something that she had never seen before. "An officer fighting to keep his patrol car on the road, it was like he was struggling against something, or someone, but she did see anyone else in his car. She watched the car for at least twenty minutes, then all of a sudden it was a gun shot, and the car started flipping until it came to rest at the bottom of a hill with the lights still flashing, and the siren was still ringing, as if it was meant for someone to find it. As Yavern approached the crashed car, she called the authorities. When they arrived, they were in awe to the sight of what they saw. They could not believe a car could be so twisted and mangled, and the person driving was still in one piece with just a single gunshot wound to his chest. Once they cut the car apart and pulled him out, Yavern could see from where she was standing that it was Deputy David Wells, the officer that shot and killed her sister Yolanda. Tears started to roll down Yavern's cheeks, she could not decipher if the tears was for relief of him constantly calling to get the family to not press charges against him, or were they tears of happiness to see this man (who shot her sister to death) dead. As she turned her head and looked down at the wreckage, she noticed an image, the image of a female that was kind-of waving at her, as she looked closer she could see that the image was her twin sister Yolanda, and at that moment she knew Yolanda had gotten even with the person that was accused of taking her life. As Yavern started to wave back, the image started to slowly disappear. At that moment Yavern knew her sister would finally be able to take her rest.

REST IN PEACE YOLANDA

Story 8

It is known all around the world that Police Officers do foul, underhanded acts behind closed doors, and have always found a way to pin it on the poor slob-of-a-man that's not in the position to fight back. This is a fiction story of what happened to a young man in a Baltimore police Station. A young Terry woods was taken into custody around July 7th because of a shooting he took part in. He sat quiet for hours before asking if he could use the bathroom. While in there he shot himself. "I guess shit happens". In that case it was not just in the toilet. It was determined that he apparently shot himself while handcuffed from behind. In any case the autopsy report determined that the gun shot was self- inflicted. That final analysis did not set well with Wood's mother, or the investigating officers. As time passed the investigation was dropped, and however woods died would get lost in the shuffle along the way. That may very well be the case for the living, but Woods was not having it that way, he was going to get even with the person, or persons who was responsible for his death. Being that he died in a bathroom stall in the police station, that is where his spirit stays until he is at peace with in his death. As time passed Terry had a good time scaring the different people that entered to use the bath room toilet. Whenever one of the officers sat down to take a crap he would flush the toilet just to annoy them, or he would unroll the toilet tissue off the roll and have it string it all over the place. This went on for about a week, and then all of a sudden the fun stopped, because the two officers he remembered carried him to the bathroom, were also the two officers responsible for his death. He could see them, but they couldn't see him. He did things behind their backs, and made one think the other one did it. For example he would touch one officer on the butt, and he turned and told the other guy not to touch him anymore. As soon as his back was turned Terry did it again, this time the officer was very upset. It made him think that his friend thought he was gay. Terry did that about two more times. They got so upset with each other until they each drew their weapons. Then began the stand down, each telling the other to drop his weapon to the point of both pulling the trigger and shot each other to death. Terry starred at the bodies on the floor, and a sigh of relief came over him. Other officers came running into the bathroom to see what had happened. They knew those were the same two officers that escorted Terry Woods to the bathroom on the night of his shooting death they wondered if the officers were somehow connected with the shooting. Even though everyone knew the shooting was a mystery as to how a handcuffed prisoner managed to enter a jail with a gun undetected, and manage to shoot himself to death while in a bathroom stall, was something they could not figure out. They may now have the missing piece of the puzzle. In any case Terry Woods spirit was finally able to leave the bathroom stall, and take his rest.

Rest in Peace Terry Woods

All of these stories are fiction, however; there are real people that have lived, and died the same as these folks, but because of their deaths have gone unsolved they are spirits of unrest, and will not rest until the persons responsible for their deaths have been caught, or the spirits gives them the punishment that they deserve.

THE END

"Lock Down"

This was the first day an eighteen old man entered prison for the first time in his life. He looked around at all the cells, the oversized men, and some other young men his age. It was not hard to tell he as scared to death. It was in his voice. His name was JaWayne. He looked up at the two security guards that was escorting him to his cell, and asked "How many people will be in my cell?" It is usually just one other person, answered one guard. "But you still have to watch your back."

As young JaWayne settled into his new temporary horne, after rneeting his new cellmate, he realized that he was another young black man t h at has gotten into the system, the state system. However; his cell mate was a white young man, around twenty five years of age, his name was Josh. JaWayne learned that Josh had been in prison since the of fifteen, and that he had been put through the wringer. He had seen his share of being mistreated as a new inmate. Although JaWayne crime was selling drugs, it still was not as bad as what Josh's crime was, which was murdering his father.

As time passed, and the cellmates got a little more comfortable with one another, they began to elaborate on their lives t o each other, and what brought them to their demise. JaWayne revealed that he was following the wrong crowd, not listening to his parents, and not staying in school. He got turned on to selling drugs by his peers because of the fast money. It started as a small amount of drugs, as little as one hundred, to two hundred dollars, minor stuff. Then out of nowhere, some older guys approached him with a bigger package, a better plan of making a lot more money. He fell for it hook, line, and sinker. At the age of seventeen, and making a thousand dollars a day was a fantasy come true for JaWayne. It was exciting at first, and then things got real. There were people trying to rob him at every turn for money and drugs. And others wanted to kill him for selling on their turf. If it was not other dealers, it was the police watching his every move. Suddenly, his life was not his own any more. He was being used stalked, and harrassed every minute of every day. Then the obvious happened, he sold to an undercover agent. That day he had at least ten thousand dollar cash money and twenty thousand in drugs on him at the time. Although JaWayne had gone to jail many times before for small stuff, this time it was different. It felt different to him. In his heart he knew he would go away for a very long time for this crime. He was right, the court gave him twenty years. To him, it would be a life time.

After JaWayne finished talking, it was josh turn to give an explanation as to what started his downfall at such a young age. He started to explain that he came from an abusive family. He remembered how his dad used to beat his mom every day, for the least little things she did. He talked about the one day he thought his mom was dead, because his dad beat her so badly that she actually stopped breathing for a minute. That lasted for as long as his mom allowed it to. Then his dad started in on him and his brothers. It started with the beatings, then the molestations, which turned into being sodomize by my own dad. And if it wasn't me, he was raping my sisters. At the time I was only like twelve years old.

"As josh continued to talk, JaWayne could not believe what he was hearing." His heart went out to Josh. But then Josh wasn't finished telling his story yet.

Josh continued his story. He went on to say that his father did all that with no remorse. His father continued to go to work, come home and act like nothing happened. Josh said that whenever his father came for him after that he started fighting back. He said he would pick up anything he could get his hands on to hit him. He also started protecting his sisters. However; he couldn't very well protect his mom from her beatings, because she wouldn't fight back, and he also felt that she didn't try to stop his dad when they were being sexually abused, so he figured she liked getting beat up so he let her.

Josh said that the abuse went on for another year or better, at least until he got really fed up, and he decided it was time to end it. He said that one night just after his thirteenth birthday his dad came home a little drunk, and started an argument with his mother. He hit her so hard she fell to the floor, and was knocked out cold. He then reached for me, I stepped back and he fell, that's when I got on top of him and began stabbing him. When I realized it I had stabbed him at least thirty times. The law said it was an over kill, and not self defense. If I had just stabbed him once, "given the past history" it would have been self-defense. Well now you know why I've been here since I was fifteen, and I still have twenty years to go. I guess some of the years are for arson, because, after I killed him, and got my sisters and mom out the house, I set it on fire. So now you know the whole story. I'm a murderer, and an arsonist.

JaWayne sat quietly and listened to everything that Josh said, and was lost for words. He could not think of anything to say to Josh except, "'I'm sorry man that you and your family went through all of that. I though my life was tough, but what you went through beats everything I went through." Then he just shakes his head while still looking at Josh. "So, Josh man; do any of your family come here to see you?" ask JaWayne.

"Yea man, for the first two years my mom came here on a regular basis, but she died the next year. As far as my sisters are concerned, they were so busy spending mom and dad's insurance money, they don't care if I lived or died. They did come to see me once after mom died just to thank me for saving their lives, and to also tell me that they would not be coming back any more, but they will write to me." But it's cool, I have made peace with myself, and my new home for the next twenty years." Josh chuckled a little after he made that statement.

"So what about you JaWayne, do you have any family that will be visiting you in here? asked Josh. Well I don't know man, I do have a mother, a brother, and a sister, but as far as them coming out here to see me, I don't think so. But why not? asked Josh. Well to begin with, they were very upset with me for being pulled into the s--- to start with, they said they thought I had better sense than that. My mom said she would never come to see me if I'm ever stupid enough to go to jail. I don't blame them man, who wants to see their loved one behind prison walls. I really regret the choice that I made to start selling drugs, especially after seeing what it did to some of my other friends. Like what man? Asked Josh. What happened to your friends? "Well my friend named Pete died of a drug overdose when he was just 13 (thirteen) years old. He somehow got into some Cocaine his older brother had under his mattress. Pete saw him put it there and thought it was flour, Pete use to love eating flour. They took him to the hospital, but he died anyway. Another one of my female friends, Amy was messing around with some dudes, whom she thought it was cool. One of them told her it would be cool for her to try something new by way of getting hi. They all shot up, and cooked her up some to try. She had never tried anything like that before, and it was too much for her, it burst her heart and she died, she was only 16 (sixteen) at the time. I never tried using the drugs, all I wanted to do is sell them just to make the money, which was a mistake that I will be paying for the next ten years." Said JaWayne.

"Well if it's of any comfort to you I'll be right here with you, for the crime I committed I'll probably be in here the rest of my life" said Josh.

"I couldn't ask for better company" said JaWayne.

The two roommates talked for hours. It seemed they had much more in common than they realized. Every day they had a new conversation on a new subject pertaining to their past lives. That went on for the next five years after that it was always some sort of conflict going on that started them fearing for their lives. One day their worst fears came to past when a new guy was transferred to the prison and for some reason started a fight with Josh and few days later and he was killed. From that day forward

JaWayne pretty much kept to himself. He eventually got a new roommate, but they never connected like him and Josh. This is a fiction tale about two young men that made wrong decisions in their lives, and it cost them dearly. If there's a young person reading this story, please think before acting on your instincts. It could save you years of agony.

THE END

A GLIMMER OF LIGHT

"in a time of hope"

From the day God created man it has been some sort of turmoil. It all started with the sons of Adam and Eve. Their names were Cain, and Able, and from that day forward, man has found a reason to go up against one another. However; the Black man has always had to fight for their rights, and even more for their lives. *As* a black man, it was not easy to make a statement, and back it up without getting knocked down, even if the statement was true. The right to speak had to be earned. It all started with white folks using blacks as slaves and calling them niggers. After the word "nigger" was no longer accepted, or used by folks, they then started calling men "boys" it didn't matter how old a man was, he was called "Boy". After the word boy became a word that was used to low rate men was no longer accepted by society, or used by slave owners, men then became "colored boys', or just colored people. The word "colored" was used by the white society to describe African Americans folks. It did not matter if your complexion was as light as theirs, and they knew you were half white, to them, you were still considered to be a colored person.

After black men became educated, and learned to speak the English language that wasn't broken to sound like "ebonies which is only a part of a word," they learned that being people of color entitled them to be called Negroes, and that gave them pride, and made them proud to stand up for what they believed in, which was their African American heritage. *As* black mer grew smarter, the white man became angrier, and more aggressive in their behavior towards Black men. It didn't take much to set them off. They did not understand how the Negroes were getting so educated. They knew the black man was not financially able go to college, and far be it for the white man to finance such a big step up for blacks, and in some ways, the white man would lose control of the situation if blacks became smarter.

When Dr. Martin Luther King Jr. came on the scene in 1955, he really began to shake things up. He told black men that they had a voice, and if they didn't know how to use their voice, he would speak for them. That's when the black man's world began to open up. They could finally see the forest through the trees. Their eyes, and ears were opened, and they were able to see, and hear as Dr. King talked with them, he cried with them, he prayed with them, he marched with them, and he went to jail with them. While they were in jail, it was like a darkness that fell upon them. They were in their cells, but there was no light. All they wanted was a "glimmer of light" to be able to read if only for a little while. The only luminance was the dim emergency lights after everything else was turned off. In the darkness was a ray of light. Each person that was jailed had the opportunity to use the light within them to get an understanding of why they were jailed, and what cause they were fighting for. They knew it was for freedom, but how is being locked up "freedom"? I guess the explanation of that will come later.

A "Glimmer of Light" is a tale of the silent cry with in us all. We need a little light in this world of darkness. When there is so much destruction, death, disease, and disrespect among our youths, blacks and whites. But, how did they get started with it all. They didn't just wake up one day and decided "today is the day we will bring destruction to the world" No, they got the idea from their surroundings, their peers, their parents, their friends or anyone that they looked up to, or wanted to pattern themselves after. The battle of white officers against black unarmed men, or as of late, black men attacking and shooting Police Officers has gotten way out of hand. It's like the Iraq war, or ISIS has come to the states. There is also the attack of the gay bar in Florida, in which 49 people died, and the shooting at the Church in Charleston in which nine people died. I can go on and on about all those people killed, but my point is all those lives mattered. They were fathers, mothers, sisters, brothers, and people that had lives, goals, dreams, and perhaps ideas to make the world a better place. When Dr. Martin Luther King Jr. marched, preached and prayed, it was not just for blacks, it was for whites as well, and any race of people that heard him speak. It is time for us to Love our neighbors as we love ourselves.

Watch out for, and take care our sisters, and our brothers. Black, white or indifferent. God loves us all. It is time to love each other as God loves us.

By Joan J. Davis/Published Author

Date: Started May 28, 2018

Story Title: Why is there Hell on Earth?

Sub Topic: "Living with demons"

As we move oh so slowly about in the twist and turns of this thing called life, it is getting harder and harder to understand that we are not in control of anything, not that we ever were. We are living with demons and they are revealing themselves to us every day. They are controlling certain individuals within their minds. Day in and day out there is some sort of controversy going on in the world. It starts when we wake up in the morning, until we go to bed at night. The majority of the conversations are about the leaders of our free world. Why is it so hard for them to make the right decisions that will help everyone live a happier, safer life? There again are signs that minds are being controlled by demons, especially when there are people in the worldly positions are only making decisions to suit their needs. With all the negatives against our world leaders I think maybe it's time the country do the right thing and evict them all out of Washington D.C. The World is going to Hell in a HANDBAG and demons are leading the way, and there's not one thing we as individuals can do about it. We have to come together as a team to make it work. There have been school shootings, church shootings, shootings of folks at music concerts. All of these incidents are the demons coming out parties. They want everyone to know they exist. We pray and ask God for his blessings every day. We even ask him to watch over our children, and keep them safely out of harms way. However; as of late it seems our prayers have gone unanswered, because there are still so many children being murdered, it's as if our prayers only reaching as high as the ceiling, and not God's ears. Have people become so demonized that everything they see is so threatening, and scary that they would rather see someone dead, or get themselves killed rather than seek help for whatever is going on within their demonized mind. Wht is being done in Washington D.C about Gun control?

Absolutely nothing that we can see . The shootings are not the only thing degrading our society, with all of the confessions of men in high profile pf)sitions admitting to drugging, and sexually assaulting women in the *w(1r.k* place in nothing to sneeze at. They are not only losing their positf.nns, but their dignity, and self respect as well. We are actually living with demons in "Hell on earth."

I was actually a drug user years ago, and during the time I was out there I ran into quite a few demons, and they showed themselves, red eyes and all. Day after day I had an encounter with one. It actually tried to kill me several times, but I prayed for God to release me from the grips of the demon, and he did. It has been 22 years and I still see sightings of their existence after all these years. Nothing has changed, whenever I watch the news there is always the same stories, school shootings, rape and murder, prison rioting, and prison breaks. It is becoming clear that we need a better system to operate the world, and get things back in track. These are only some of the issues that is being controlled by people with demonized spirits. Another issue that has the world buzzing with fear are police officers around the world that seem to have possession of a demonized spirit. If that's not the case, then why have so many men, and women been killed by law enforcement in some way without remorse? It's like they're shooting first, and asking questions later. It's like demons are reveiling themselves in any, and every aspect, which tell us that we're living in the last days of revelations. It tells us what to expect from life and we are experiencing it every day. The drug dealers have gone from selling to using. They have gone from cocaine, to prescribed pain medications, and that has become a real problem for the people that has severe pain, and is in need of the medication. The drug companies are coming down very hard on the Doctors, and they're coming down hard on us "the patients". This world is changing so dramatically, to where it is barely recognizable anymore. I remember the time when myself, and other children looked forward to going to school, saying the Pledge of Allegiance, the Our Fathers Prayer, and beginning our learning experience for the day with friends. In even remembered my own children being excited about going to school. That was 12 years ago, I know because that's how long it's been since my baby daughter graduated High School. However; that is no longer a happy experience for school children today. Today it is a matter of just staying alive, and getting through the day. It is a sad, sad life when little children cannot even focus on learning, they actually spend their day practicing staying safe. There so many issues that I can speak on relating to demonizing behavior, but there is not enough hours in the day. As a writer I have had the opportunity to speak to some of the youths in Elementary, Middle, and High School. It is amazing to me of how many school age children ask questions pertaining to drug life, a life in prison, or would it be hard to learn how to shoot a gun. One child said he loved watching movies with a lot of shooting in it, and when the show is over he acts out the scenes by running around the house shooting with his fingers. Many of the children said they want to be a Police Officer when they grow up just so they could shoot a gun legally. I did not quite know how to answer them right away, but as I thought about it the answers started to pour out. I told them that once you've aimed a gun at someone and pulled a trigger there's no way to stop a bullet once it's left the chamber, and at that very moment you realize that you've made a big mistake, one that may cost you your very own life. The children listened very intensely, absorbing every word that I was saying to them. After I finished my speech, they started asking questions again, but this time they were questions that mattered. Such as "what can they do to make a difference in the world"? They now want to become Lawyers, Doctors, and Judges. One kid said that he would like to run for president someday, but not like the present world leaders, more like the past leaders. The news reports also have a way of influencing children's mind and their behavior. For instance when a child sees that another child has done something such as shooting up a school, they have a preconceived idea that they could do it as well. In some ways, it pays not advertise.

I don't know how or even if the country can be fixed. It is so broken with all the insane things people to one another in this world, but I know something has to be done to stop the corrupt behavior. There, again are signs of Demonic behavior. I do know that whatever is going on with our world leaders needs to stop long enough to come to some kind of consensus about a stronger gun law. I have walked down the streets in my neighborhood and down the isles in the malls and seen the impression of a gun barrel in the pants of some men clothing. I did not give any clues that I had seen the gun, however; from the look on my face I'm sure they had an idea that I knew something. By the time I had gotten to the sub Police station in the Mall to tell them what I had seen, the young men had left the store. There is something about the blank stare on a young *man's* face, and the emptiness in his eyes that says "I don't care about anyone, or anything" he has no soul, and he lives by the orders of demons. I have written about "Demons" from the beginning of this story, that's because

I strongly feel that there are demons living within our spirits. If not, then what is making people do the things they do. It is certainly not the spirit of God, because God don't put thoughts of murder, rape, and other ungodly ideas in people's heads.

This is a dog eat dog world, and everyone must look out for themselves. In go to church every Sunday and I don't hear the preacher preach "the Gospel, you hear him preach the Gossip, which is something that he experienced the week before, which no one wants to hear about. I thank God for being God because he helps us to understand beyond that.

It really does not matter where we go in the world, there will always be the presence of demons, but they will be unrecognizable because they stand, walk upright, talk, and act just like a regular man. They are very hard to spot. They could be right in front of you plotting their next move and you will never know it. We are fighting a demonic war every day that we will never win. We are living in Hell on Earth from now until the day we die, and then we will go and be with the Lord in Heaven.

THE END

The "Bully" of a Halloween Horror

"Fiction"

It all started at school, a school of mixed race. There were blacks, white, Latinos, and Mexicans. This school had it all. There are at least 1500 children in this large school, which sits in the middle of a small town in Rocky Mount North Carolina. The grades in the school are from first through the twelfth. Most of the boys in the higher grades are built, very muscular, and very strong. They played football, basketball, or they wrestled. The other boys in the same grades were considered to be geeks to them and they were pushed around, and bullied a lot.

Narrator: There were at least five boys that hung together all the time, one of them of course, was a geek, and he hung with other boys to be popular with the girls. This school had it all, a different race of people. Some were Black, White Latino, Mexican, and a few was mixed, white and Mexican, and Black and White. Every weekend these five boys would get together for a new adventure, and most of the time it was trouble. Their names were Frank, Pete, Roland, Brian, and Rodriguez. In this small town in North Carolina, there was once a rumor of either a wild dog, or a werewolf that was killing some animals, and once in a while a person was found torn all to pieces. It was the story that Mr. McPherson was always telling people. On this particular Saturday night, these five boys decided to take a walk to do some exploring down by a rail road track. As they walked, they noticed pieces of animal carcass scattered all over the tracks. However, that did not stop them, they kept on walking. The more they walked, the more afraid they become. Being the bullies they were, they dared the geek boy "Pete" to walk out in front of them, at least ten feet ahead, to be exact. He was told that if he didn't do it, he would not be able to hang out with them anymore.

"Pete" said Brian, (the leader in the group) I need you to walk way out in front and yell back and tell us if you see anything strange, ok!

Ok Brian! Said Pete, (as if he was trying hard to please the gang leader).

Narrator: they walked several more miles, not realizing that Pete was so far ahead, he was actually out of sight. Rodriguez was the first one to yell to Pete.

Pete! Yo Pete, man where are you? Ask Rodriguez.

"Yea man", wait up for us," said Frank.

Brian! Said Roland, "Why did you bully him to walk ahead of us like that? I sure hope he's alright".

"Me too man." Said Brian.

(As they continued to walk, they continued to call out to Pete)

Pete! Where you at man? Said Frank and Roland almost at the same time, and then they dabbed fist feeling good about thinking alike. They were all kind of talking among themselves when all of a sudden they heard a howl.

What the hell was that? Asked Brian. It sounded like a howl! Said Rodriguez.

It sure did! Said Frank.

I'm ready to get the hell away from here, said Roland.

I'm with you there bud, said Brian, but not before we find Pete!

Narrator: They took a few more steps and came upon an old shed that sat alongside the railroad tracks. They also encountered the worse smell ever. As they got closer they could clearly see an animal eating something. When they peeked around the animal, (trying not to make any noise) they recognized it as Pete that was being eaten, but what was eating him was unclear; it looked like a dog, but when it stood up it was bigger than a dog, it was hairy with long claws, and big teeth. At that moment they realized the rumor about the werewolf was true. They all stared at it. Their feet were frozen in place. They each looked down just in time to see the partially eaten remains of what was once their friend. They all started to scream, and finally started running, first in the same direction, then they decided to split up into different directions. The werewolf started in behind them, but settled for the one that was closest. It was Brian.

"Help me guys, he's got me!" yelled Brian. Please don't let him kill me.

"Man I told you we should not have come this far from home", said Rodriguez.

"You're right man," said Frank. I wonder which way Roland went! I don't know, but I sure hope he makes it.

"Me too man," said Rodriguez.

NARRATOR: As Frank and Rodriguez walked a little further, they walked deeper into the woods, and the smells got worse.

"Damn man, where are we?" asked Rodriguez.

"It sure smells bad in here!" said Frank.

NARRATOR: All of a sudden they heard someone breathing fast, as if out of breath from running. When they ask "is someone out here?" out popped Roland from where he was hiding which was a little shack. Somehow they has wandered even deeper into the woods, and perhaps stumbled upon the werewolf's storage area, the place where he keeps his left over carcass. While the boys was trying to figure out where they were, the sound of the wolf howling was really close. They looked at each other, and ran to hide again. This time they went into a little closet in the shack. They listened for the sound of more howling. It was quiet for a moment, and that gave them enough time to talk about Brian and what happened to him.

"Man do you think the werewolf ate him?" ask Frank.

"I don't know man," said Roland, I just know I was scared as hell!

"Me too," said Rodriguez I just wish this was a bad joke someone is playing on us, especially since it's Halloween and all.

"I don't think this is a joke dude!" said Frank. "I think that animal out there is real, and if Brian is dead he deserved it, being such a bully, bullying Pete like that.

"Yea man, poor Pete, he didn't deserve to die like that, and neither do we." Said Rodriguez. What we need are some weapons. Let's see what we can find in here. We need a gun and some silver bullets! (they chuckle at the sound of that.) Then they looked at each other as if saying that may not be a bad idea, after all they has read that werewolves can be killed with silver bullets.

Roland spoke first, "So what are we going to do dudes, stay in this closet all night, or are we going to make a run for it."

"I don't know man! Said Frank, do you really think it's gone?"

"I sure hope so." Said Rodriguez.

NARRATOR: They emerged from closet slowly, one at a time, as if trying not to make any noise. They eased their way to the door, opening it slowly and peeking out, but they suddenly realized they didn't have a plan as to how they would get away.

"Let's try and stick together," suggested Rodriguez, and we could maybe get to the railroad tracks and then run like hell all the way home.

"That sounds like a plan to me," said Frank! "We better hurry because it may have family around here that he's feeding with all this dead meat."

Just as three boys started out the door a werewolf jumped out from the woods, they begun to run, however, one boy, Roland was not quite fast enough. The werewolf reached for him and knocked him off balanced, he lost his footing and fell, before he knew it the werewolf was in top of him, clawing and biting him, he started screaming louder, and louder, but the other boys, (two of the original five) just kept running, they assumed that since the werewolf was preoccupied with Roland that was their chance to get away. Once Roland was out cold, the werewolf started for the other boys, he reached out to grab one, but was only able to scratch one of them, and that was Frank. Once they started running they didn't stop until they got home. They were so out of breath, to the point of not being able to talk.

After they finally caught their breaths, they looked at each other in silent. They were trying to adjust their thoughts to what they had just witnessed only few hours ago. All of a sudden Frank started to feel the scratch on his back. He was running so fast he didn't realize that he was hurt.

"Man do you think what we just went through was real?" ask Frank.

"I'm trying to remember man, but some of it seems like a blur, it didn't seem real. But, what happened to Pete, Brian, and Roland?" Asks Rodriguez.

"Man we have to tell somebody! Someone that will believe us, man this scratch on my back hurts! I need to get it looked at before it gets worst." Said Frank.

"Somebody like who?" Ask Rodriguez. You mean somebody like that old man, the one that started telling us about the werewolf, you know Mr. McPherson.

"Yeah! Let's go tell him about it, and see what he has to say!" Answered Rodriguez.

"Yeah! And we still have to explain what happened to Brian, Pete, and Roland. Damn this scratch hurts like hell." Said Frank.

NARRATOR: They finally caught their breaths, and decided to go visit Mr. McPherson, but on the way Frank decided to go by the hospital to get his back looked after. Once he got in to see the nurse she was frightened at the sight of the wound. The first thing the doctor asked Frank was "where did you get this scratched?" Frank starts to answer but he looked over at Rodriguez, and from the look on Rodriguez's face, he wasn't sure if Frank should tell the truth, or not to tell the truth, in any case there must be an answer as to where the scratches came from. The doctor continued to clean the wound, and then began stitching it up. The entire time Frank whined like a baby. As the Doctor stitched, he continued to question Frank as to how he received such large scratches.

"They must hurt like chicken," said the Doctor.

"Yeah! You're not lying Doc," said Frank.

When the pain killers finally set in, and Frank began to relax a little, he started talking.

"I'll tell you Doc, but you may not believe what I tell you," said Frank.

Frank began to tell the Doctor what happened.

"It all started when me, and my friends decided to go for a walk down the rail road tracks. It was actually decided by the "bully gang leader Brian" (who is dead now), anyhow; we started walking further, and further down the tracks. Hold on, Doc you heard the rumor about a wild dog, or some wild animal that's been killing things and people right?" The doctor nodded as if intrigued at what Frank was saying.

"Well any way, Brian was the leader and he "bullied Pete."

"Yea! Interrupted Rodriguez, he made Pete walk way out in front of the rest of us."

"Can I finish telling the story now Rodriguez, or do you want to tell it?" asked Frank.

"Go head man," said Rodriguez

"Like he said, Brian made Pete walk ahead of us, he was so far ahead we lost sight of him, and we began to call out to him, but he didn't answer. We just kept walking and finally we walk up on an animal that was eating something. At first we thought it was a dog, but as we got closer to it we could see it clearer, then it stood up and we saw that it was eating Pete. It was real tall, and it started howling like a werewolf. We started to run but it grabbed Brian. Then me, Rodriguez, and Roland ran and hid in an old shack for a while, and when we thought the coast was clear we ran back down the tracks toward home, and that's when it got Roland, and scratched me. So what do you think about that story Doc? asked Frank.

"That's a hell-of-a-story I must admit, but it lines up with this scratch you got, but, a werewolf? Here in Rocky Mountain North Carolina! That's hard to believe. Now about this scratch, don't let it get infected, or you'll have trouble on your hands." said the doctor.

"I don't know about trouble, but I know it hurts like hell Doc. How many stitches you had to put in it? Ask Frank.

"About thirty," said the doc.

"Doc, are you going to tell the police or somebody about what happened to Pete, Brian, and Roland? Ask Rodriguez, cause if you don't I guess me and Frank will have to do it."

"Well I guess I can talk to Sheriff Sims, and maybe talk to Mr. McPherson, cause he's the one that started that rumor, so he might know something. Then somebody has to explain to those boys families about what happened to them. I guess the Sheriff can do that too. I suppose he'll go out and investigate everything." said Doc.

"Hey Doc, you think I got anything to worry about with this scratch, like maybe turning into a werewolf?" ask Frank.

"I don't know son, if it was a wolf I've heard that you may show some symptoms, but I don't know how true it is. I guess you'll just have to wait and see." Answered Doc.

"In the mean time I guess I need to go home and rest, come on Rod." Said Frank.

NARRATOR: Both Rodriguez and Frank began to walk home very slowly, as if regretting going there. The memory of their friends rests on their minds. They tried desperately to understand what happened to them and their friends, when they were just hanging out only 24 hours ago. It was like a nightmare that they couldn't wake up from. They hadn't thought about how they would explain everything to the other kids at school, or to the boy's parents for that matter.

"Frank do you remember everything that happened last night? asked Rodriguez."

"Yeah man, I do," answered Frank, but I still cannot believe they're all gone. Brian, Pete, and Roland, they're all gone.

NARRATOR: They both started to sniff as if they began to cry, and then all of a sudden wiped their eyes so the other one wouldn't see him crying. Meanwhile; the sheriff, his deputies, and a group of volunteers decided to investigate, and they all went werewolf hunting. They went to the area the boys described to the doctor, but the only thing they discovered was a bad smell, a few bones, and some clothing which they gathered up for evidence. When they got back to town they called the two boys to come to the police department to identify the clothing that they found. When Frank and Rodriguez got there, they immediately ran to the clothes they saw on the desk, that's when they both started to cry out loud. They pulled themselves together after a few minutes, enough to ask the police if they found the werewolf, when the police said no, they dropped their heads, and ask if they could go back home. When the boys left, the police realized that those boys had been through a lot in the past 48 hours. A few months passed and the memory of how their friends died was a fuzzy memory. However; Frank started to feel some of the affects from the scratch he received the night his friends died.

"Yo Rod man, I've been feeling real funny lately. My hearing has gotten keener, my sight is much better, and I can run faster" Said Frank.

"Frank you could always run fast, that's why you're the running back on the team, and you never complained about your sight or hearing" stated Rodriguez.

"You're right man, but everything is keener now. I've gotten stronger, and I can smell the donut shop from all the way across town" said Frank.

"Damn man, said Rodriguez, do you think it came from scratch you got months ago?"

"I don't know Rod, but I'll find out on the next full moon, which is in about two weeks" said Frank.

NARRATOR: Frank didn't realize it, but all the symptoms he's been experiencing are all leading to him becoming the next werewolf in Rocky Mount N.C. As time passed, and it got closer to the moon becoming full, the more Frank felt the changes. He started losing his teeth and hair, his fingernails and toenails started to grow and get harder, and he still didn't want to admit that something was wrong. His mood began to change at school. He began to get meaner toward everyone. His friend Rod even asked him what was going on with him, especially after he noticed his mood swings.

"Hey Frank what's up man? Asked Rod, why don't we hook up later man and go for some pizza, ok. We haven't seen each other in a while, and I miss you buddy. So what do you think?"

NARRATOR: Frank answered Rod without looking up from what he was doing.

"No! Answered Frank, I got some other stuff going right now."

NARRATOR: When Frank finally looked up at Rid, he was frightened at the sight of his best friend. The look Frank had in his eyes was the look of a wild animal. Something that Rod did not recognize. It did not look like his friend at all.

"Alright man, said Rod, just asking. I'll see you later alright. You need to get some rest man because you loom tired.

NARRATOR: Rod walked away shaking his head, wondering what has happened to his best friend.

"I saw three of my friends died at the hands of a werewolf and it looks like my last friend is becoming one." Said Rodriguez.

NARRATOR: Later that night Rod decided to go by Frank's house to check on him. However, on his way there he looked up to see that the moon was full. As he approached the door he heard some weird noises coming from the back of the house. As he moved forward to investigate, an animal suddenly ran past him. It was moving very fast. He ran for it, but disappeared into the darkness. Shortly afterwards he heard a howl that sounded like what he remembered that night two months ago. He proceeded to the door. He knocked and called out to Frank.

"Frank, are you in here?"

NARRATOR: When Frank didn't answer, Rod went in the house, and what he saw has him believe that a wild animal was in there. Because things were thrown everywhere. He just shook his head and walked back out the door. He started to wonder if Frank was the new werewolf in town. While Rodriguez sat alone in his car, his mind went back to Brian and how he use to bully them, and push them around so much, especially

Pete who just wanted to be part on the group. It was Brian that talked them into walking down the tracks in the first place. Rod realizes that he survived a brutal attack that took the lives of all of his friends, although Frank is still alive, his life is forever changed, and now Rod has to start making new friends, but he will never forget his old friends Brian, Pete, Roland, and Frank.

The Unfaithful Wife

"Fiction"

Short Story

There's a time in this married couple's life when all they have is each other, and the vows they spoke when they got married. They each have great jobs, and that's what kept them occupied, until the birth of their first child two years later. A little girl named "Santana". After she was born, she became the center of their attention. They each took turns doing their parental duties, at least for a while. Samantha was a paralegal at a large law firm. Her husband Josh was a "well known" Attorney with a different law firm. As most couples are in the first few years, they were happy, open and honest. However in the last couple of years that has changed. They have grown apart.

Josh has a brother "Joseph" that was also an attorney at the same laws firm that his wife Samantha works at. As time passed, Josh duties with their daughter grew. It was obvious that he was the after school care giver. He was responsible for picking her up from school, giving her dinner and putting her to bed. Though he had all of these extra duties with his baby, he did not mind, because his daughter is his heart. Josh realizes that his wife has a job that requires her to work late on occasions, but he didn't expect it every day. He did not become skeptical about her late hours until she started coming home later than 8:00 pm. One night it was 10:00 pm, and soon after that she got home midnight. That was the straw that broke the camel's back. He decided to confront her.

"Samantha, why have you been coming home so late at night?" Asked Josh. "Have you forgotten that we have a daughter that has to be cared for, she needs her mother."

"Yes Josh! I know we have a daughter, but I also have a job that requires me to work late some nights, and other nights I go out and have drinks with my girlfriends." Stated Samantha.

"I can understand you working late some nights Samantha, but every night is kind of ridiculous! Said Josh. But if that is the case, then it would be courteous if you could give me a call to let me know what's going on." Said Josh.

Narrator: As time passed things got a little better for Josh and Samantha. They both started coming home at a reasonable time, and once again shared responsibility of their child. However, after about a month, the same things started to happened, except this time instead of Samantha not picking up the baby, she would pick her up and carried her to her grandmother's house, (which is Josh's mother) and picks her up later and bring her home. That didn't quite work out because the baby was still being picked up late, and put to bed late. When Josh realized what was happening, he once again confronted his wife. This time he have her an ultimatum that either she will carry out her duties with her child, she will have to quit her job. He told her that she cannot be married, a mother, and have her freedom to do just what shew wanted to do.

When Samantha heard those ultimatums, she flipped out. She went off on Josh in flash. What do you mean, "I will have to quit my job." So, you're saying that I cannot be a mother, have a job, a life, and be married to you at the same time? Is that's what you are saying Josh?

Because it sure sounds like it. Well let me tell you something Josh, I never told you that I would be bare-foot-and-pregnant wife. Of course I want, and love our daughter, but the responsibility is ours, Josh, not just mine. Now, in the future I will call and let you know if I have to work late so you can pick up the baby from daycare. I may also go and have drinks with my friends some time, because I need some "me" time Josh, and I'll expect you to do the same thing if you want to hang out with your friends. Come on baby we can work this out.

Josh stood there looking at the woman that she loves so much, and realized that he was being selfish in what he wanted, and he began to apologize to her.

"I'm sorry baby, for being selfish. Asking you to quit your job was taking things a bit too far. I do believe you can be a mother and have a career. But, all I ask of you is make a little for our daughter. I don't mind picking her up some of the time, and putting her to bed, but she also needs her mother to put her to bed at proper time, and not all times a night."

Samantha shook her head in agreement with what Josh said.

"Ok baby, I can do that. I promise to be more responsible. I just got a little carried away with the time, but it won't happen again."

Narrator: As time went on, Samantha did as she promised for a while. She picked up the baby from the day care, took her home, fed her, bathed her, and even read her a bedtime story before putting her to bed. She did everything that Josh expected her to do. And he was very pleased at her efforts. However that lasted for about a month, and she was right back up to her old tricks. Josh's mother started picking up the baby, after being asked by Samantha. Josh didn't understand the sudden change, so he decided to investigate her at her job. It was ten o'clock at night, and he wondered where Sam was. He decided to go to her job, the office where she worked, which is the firm where his brother has his office. He used the key that Samantha had given him for an emergency. As he entered the office he noticed a young girl sitting at a desk. He asked, "Have you seen my wife Samantha here lately?"

Yes Sir Mr. Josh she's been working upstairs since around five o'clock!

"Upstairs ah, answered Josh, well I think I'll just surprise her."

As Josh approached the office upstairs he could hear talking, but it was in whispering tone, and he didn't know which office it was coming from. But, as he got closer, he could tell it was coming from his brother's office. The curtain was not drawn so any one that's in the hall can see inside clearly. And what Josh saw left him in shock, he knew it might have been another man, but he had no idea it was his brother that Samantha was having an affair with. He stood there at the window for a good ten minutes before they came up for air, got their barring, and realized he was watching them. Joseph, his brother spotted him first, and then he notified Samantha that they were being watched. The look on her face were both surprise, and fear. She was lost for words. She quickly began to dress as fast as she could in order to catch Josh as he walked back down the hall. When she caught up to him she tried to explain, but all he did was stare at her. Then he spoke saying, "You both will be sorry" and he just walked away. Samantha was left standing in the hallway shaking, not knowing what to think or do.

When she was finally able to move, she went back to Joseph's office and gathered the rest of her belongings, and without saying anything she just ran out the office, got into her car and started driving. She drove around for a while, until she got tired and decided to go home. When she got there, she saw that Josh had not gotten home yet, which gave her some time to think of what she wanted to say. What she didn't realize was that Josh was over at his mother's saying good bye to his mother and his daughter, because what he was about to do he knew he would not see them for a while. When he finally left his mother's house, he looked into the glove box of his car to see if he had his hand gun. He took it out to see if it had bullets in it. He then went home to find Samantha sitting in a corner chair, looking as if she has been crying. He looked at her, told her to stand up, and said "I told you that you both will pay" and he shot her in both of her knees. He did not want her dead, but, just to suffer. He left there and on his way back to his brother's office he called "911" and sent them to his home. When he arrived at his brother's office, he saw that his car was still there. He got out and started up stairs, but as he got closer he once again heard loud talking, this time it was Joseph and his wife that was arguing. He heard his brother say that the business had been bad, and his marriage was on the rocks, and he knew his wife wanted a divorce, and he did not want to live any more with those conditions, and all of a sudden the sound of gunfire riddled the building. When Josh got to the door, he saw that Joseph had shot first, his wife, and then himself. As Josh stood looking down at them, he realized that his brother was much more troubled than he realized. He dialed 911 and left. He didn't even check to see if they were dead or alive. He just left.

On his way back home, he stopped by a park, got out of his car, and sat on the park bench. He sat there for hours thinking about what he had done, and what he had witnessed. He started to cry, wondering how things could have gotten so bad. How could his marriage have gone so far of the grid? He began to talk to himself, "I gave her everything she wanted, all I ask her to do was take care of our home, and our daughter. Now look what she made me do. My brother and his wife are probably dead, all because she didn't want to stand on her marital vows. Well, (while wiping her eyes) what's done is done. Now I'll have to face the music.

Josh finally decided to dispose of the gun. He threw it into a drain pipe at the edge of the park. He got into his car and just sat there for at least five minutes. He gripped the steering wheel so tight, his knuckles started turning white. He finally started driving toward home, but changed his mind at the last minute, and decided to go to his mother's house to see his daughter, and to tell his mother what has happened. When he got there he saw that it was covered with police cars. He assumed they were looking for him, and he had already prepared himself mentally, and emotionally for what was about to transpire. He got out of the car and started walking slowly toward the house. When he got close enough to be seen, someone spotted him. There he is, there's Josh. I wonder if he knows what happened.

"Josh, his mother yelled, "the police are here looking for you. Do you know that Samantha has been shot? She's not dead, but her knees have been shot completely off."

"Yes mom, answered Josh, so has Joseph, and his wife been shot, and they're both dead.

"What do you mean they're both dead?" said his mother.

"I mean it was murder/suicide mom. I mean Joseph shot his wife and turned the gone on himself. I saw it from the outside of his office window. The same window I watched him and Sam, my wife, making love earlier, and I believe Joseph's wife saw them as well. She may have followed Samantha home and shot her, and then went back to Joseph's office to confront him, and I guess this is where it led.

"You mean to tell me that your wife and Joseph were having an affair? All this time when she was coming to pick up the baby so late, she was with Joseph. Oh my God, and now my son is dead. Well, at least Samantha was not killed, she was just shot in her knees. I guess who shot her didn't want her to walk anymore.

"Mom how is my daughter? Where is she?"

"She's in the bed asleep Josh. Just let her sleep, she has not been put to bed this early in a long while."

"Ok mom I'll leave her for the night. I guess I'll go to the hospital and check on Sam."

Police: Are you the husband of the woman that was shot in the knees over on Wates Drive, near the bay? She goes by the name Samantha?"

"Yes I'm the one! But I don't really know what happened. My theory is that my wife is having an affair with my brother, and his wife got wind of it, and one thing led to another. I think she went to my house to confront my wife. I don't know why she shot her in the knees. Well, when she left there, she then went to Joseph's office, they argued, struggled, and he shot her, and then himself, at least that's what I think happened.

Narrator: When Josh left his mother's house, he headed to the hospital to see Samantha. Even though he knew exactly what happened to Samantha, or the part he played in her being shot, he just wanted to see just how much she remembered. When he reached her room he was shocked to see the condition she was in. Because the way the bullets shattered her knees, both of her legs had to be amputated above the knees. He stared at her for some time before he attempted to let her know he was in the room. He suddenly came back to reality and walked over to her bed side. He spoke in a voice which he seem to be fighting back tears.

"Hello Samantha, it's me Josh."

Narrator: Samantha tried to say something but her throat was a little dry from all the medication they had been giving her. Then she finally opened her eyes, and looked at Josh as if seeing her for the first time. When she finally spoke, she asked Josh who he was. It seemed that she had lost her memory. Josh asked her if she remembered what happened to her. In her drowsy state she said she thought she was in an accident or some kind. Josh could no longer hold back the tears. They started to roll down his cheeks. The more he wiped, the more they fell. Josh finally pulled himself together enough to talk to Samantha.

"Samantha I'm sorry this happened to you. I never intended for things to get this far out of hand and I know you never expected this either."

Narrator: Samantha looked at him as if trying to understand what he was talking about. As far as she knew she just had an accident in her and everything else was very confusing.

"I guess I'll explain everything that happened to you the next time I come to see you. You seem to be very sleepy right now, so I'll see you later ok."

Narrator: When Josh left Samantha's bed side at the hospital that day he never looked back. He went to his mother's house, picked up his daughter and left. He moved to another town, filed for divorce, and started new life. He wanted to get as far away from Samantha, and the whole situation of what happened. He wanted it all behind him. A year later he met someone, remarried, and started a new family. He now has his own law firm, and his new wife is his law partner.

“Poetry for Life”

THE MASK

When you're trying to find something you cannot see.
Look behind the mask you might see me.

I'm the one performing, being someone I'm not.
Seeking, wanting and asking for a lot.

So much I want, but, I do not deserve.
How dare I ask, where do I get the nerve.

Mistreating so many that I meet along the way,
And not helping anyone day after day.

Not realizing that times has changed, I'm still living in the past,
You want to see reality, try looking behind the mask.

You may see double, two of the same face,
They may try and split, and move to another place.

The mask is just a cover to hide one true self,
try showing a little dignity, what little you have left.

The world is surely changing, getting worse very fast,
No one will see me change, because I'm hiding behind the mask.

Try lending a hand, or maybe showing a smile,
and the world may get better, after a while.

Right now it's in turmoil, sinking deeper in sin,
Because you're hiding out, not trying to come in.

Try looking into your mirror it just might look back,
and you will see a true image, that's a fact.

No lovelier vision you will see, now it's time to ask,
For the sake of the world, come from behind the mask.

THE BROKEN DREAM

Wake up! Wake up from that sound sleep
you've been tossing and turning all night,
It's all the night mares you're having and
broken dreams that causing a fright.

You sit up and look around the darkness
to see if everything looks the same,
You put your face in the palm of your hands
you know the troubles of the day is the blame.

You see shadows peering through the window
There are shapes, and figures, and things,
Your imagination runs away with you
You even see things with wings.

The Broken Dream toys with your mind
You try, but you cannot make it go away,
You lay your head back on the pillow
and what comes to mind is what happened yesterday.

It's not the first time this has happened
It happens again, and again.
It causes you to have sleepless nights,
And leaves your body racked with pain.

Broken dreams are often messages
It comes in loud and clear,
You can't ever figure it out, or put it together
And it always leaves you in fear.

More often than not some dreams are scary
And sometimes broken dreams come true,
If you dream a dream and it leaves you smiling
That broken dream is for you.

PLEASE DON'T SHOOT ME

(I'm your friend)

Stop young man don't shoot that gun
Maybe you're board and just looking for fun.
Don't you realize that a gun is not a Toy
And now you've used it to kill a little boy.

Not only did you destroy him
But your life is over now too.
Now the law and his family
will be coming after you.

You will try to run
And you will try to hide
But your conscious want let you rest
And it will take you for a ride

You cannot shake the feeling
That what you did was wrong,
So you run, and you run,
and you run, all night long.

You finally get to lie down
But your mine won't let you sleep
Because the life you took was once your friend
Now all you can do is weep.

So weep little man, cry if you will
Until God speaks to your heart
And says
"My child peace be still"

THE BLACKBIRD

(Ecstasy)

**Watch out for the Blackbird, it will come after you.
It will help you to drown your sorrows, and ease your pains too.**

**It will lift up your spirits, and put you on top of the world,
It will put that gleam in your eyes, and your head will start to swirl.**

**Don't stop to look behind you, or take the time to rest,
Thinking the Blackbird will leave you alone and return to its nest.**

**It's not that easy to sway, once it start flapping its wings
It rises higher and higher and suddenly it will spring.**

**It has roving eyes like a hawk, and the brain of a bald eagle,
It will find you wherever you go, much like a trained beagle.**

**It preys on the weak minds, and the minds that's gone astray,
It lurks around every corner, looking from day to day.**

**The Blackbird is "Ecstasy" it destroys, and it will kill,
It's a substance folks use until their desire is fulfill.**

**So don't get caught by the Blackbird, or you will discover,
That it will take you so far down, and you may never recover.**

"LISTEN"

Listen! Can't you hear the crying in your ear?
The sound of my blood crying from the ground
Just seconds after you shot me down.

Now listen to my heartbeat, you don't hear it anymore,
All because you got angry, and wanted to settle a score.

You've taken me from my parents, siblings, and friends too,
just because I turned and walked away from you.

I heard the sound of the bullet as it left the chamber,
That horrid sound you should always remember.

I'm not there to remind you, of what you did to me,
The memory is still in your mind, and later you will see.

The toll it will take on your life as it stands,
This memory will still be there when you become a man.

Now listen to the sounds as they replay in your mind,
The pain will become so great, you'll want to leave them behind.

No matter how hard you try, you will not let it go,
And it will stay within your soul, buried deep, deep down below.

SING LITTLE BIRDIE

Chirp little Birdie, sing your heart desire,
The sound of your chirping is so admired.

The flapping of your tiny wings, is music to my ears,
The sight of you soaring the sky, just fill my eyes with tears.

You soar higher, and higher, flying into the night,
Until your tiny wings are completely out of sight.

Now, there goes your family, flying the other way,
flying in groups trying to find a warmer day.

Flying to the south by a greater number,
making their way to weather like summer.

Singing and chirping, making a musical sound,
as you fly in circles going round and round.

Stopping only to feed every once in a while,
as you perched on a bird feeder, and making a child smile.

DON'T HURT ME-*(I'M ONLY A CHILD)*

Please don't hurt me, I haven't lived yet,
I'm just a baby, my life is not set.

Please give me a chance, as someone gave you,
Let me live to do the same things that you do.

I will not cause any trouble, I'll be a good child,
Just let me live and you will see, I'll leave after a while.

Give me the love I deserve, to help me grow and mature,
And I will make you proud of me, of that I'm sure.

Don't leave me alone with someone you don't know.
You don't know what will happen when you walk out the door.

Take the time to teach me right from wrong,
Don't tarry around, or take too long.

I don't want to grow up hanging with the wrong crowd.
NOW PLEASE DON'T DESERT ME, I SAY OUT LOUD.

DON'T ABANDON ME

(I'M YOUR CHILD)

A child looks up for you to catch his hand
Not that he cannot walk or stand
He only wants you to lead, because you can.

He looks at you and smile, as only a child could
He wants you to love him and hug him
As only a mother would.

When he walks away with someone else
And he looks back at you
His eyes says "come and get me mommy"
I love you too.

But you go in another direction
Away from the path of your child
Now he sits and he waits,
He just sits and waits, he sits and waits a while.

His eyes search each face, as people pass
Hoping you'll soon appear by chance
Just so he could get a little glance.

He just want to see you, and your smile
And to catch a whiff of your smell,
and that child at that moment
can always tell.

That his mommy would never leave him
Or go very far away
And that he would be home forever, And there he would stay.

THE MOTHERLESS CHILD

Are you my mother, said the child
As he looked up, while drinking from a
child like safety cup.
Were you there when I was born?
Studying the old woman's eye s
looking sad and worn.
Did you carried me home from the hospital
Wrapped all warm and tight?
hugging me, and holding me with all your might?
Are you the one that changed my clothes
when they became soiled, washed me,
powered me, with lotion and oil.
Are you the one that sat up with me
when I became ill, or when I lost
control and made a spill.
Were you there when I started to crawl,
and eventually walked, or babbled a little
and then started to talk.
Were you there when I started with the pottie,
or occasionally soiled my pants being nottie.
Were you there when I started the first grade,
Was I scared, and started to cry, especially
when you started to wave bye, bye.
I remember you being there when
I left elementary school, and started Junior High
I remembered being very scared that I cannot deny.
I remember my first dance, and you choosing
my first suite to wear, and I did not complain,
I did not dare.
I remember the day that I graduated
You were right there with camara in hand,
And with that happy mother stare.
You have always been there

Every step on the way,
So I know you've been a mother to me
to this very day.
I don't know my real mothers name,
Or even how she looks,
There is not a letter or a picture
in any of my books.
I guess you are my mother, because you've
taken care of me
And if it was not for you,
I don't know where I would be.

"NO HOPE"

Life without hope is not dope, and it ain't no joke.

We feel the strain of life with such bitterness and strife.

The joy one gets from running, laughing, and being free, we forget sometimes that Blessings comes when we fall to our knees. There's something lacking in us all when we lose control,
when it's better to slow down and breath, so I'm told.

It is better to live today, than to worry about tomorrow, it is better to live happy than to bury our sorrow.
Take care ofyourselfand your family, and each generation you build adds to the family tree.
So live your life with hope even when life gets you down, and the hope that's in your heart will help keep your feet on the ground.

Printed in the United States
By Bookmasters